
★

"Your friends are going to have a long wait," she said.

"What do you mean by that?"

"I mean I locked the deadbolt on the apartment door and hid the key."

"You're kidding, of course," Liz said.

The woman shook her head. "This is no joke. Clover and I have both been betrayed by someone we trusted. Poor Clover can't get even, but I can. I'm going to keep you here until your friends feel as betrayed as I do—until they feel they can't trust you."

This can't be happening, Liz thought. She tried to steady her voice. "You don't want to do this. Get the key and unlock the door and we'll forget about it."

The woman only looked at her with that strange smile and shook her head.

★

DOUBLE
DECEPTION

Dorothy P. O'Neill

W⊕RLDWIDE.

TORONTO • NEW YORK • LONDON
AMSTERDAM • PARIS • SYDNEY • HAMBURG
STOCKHOLM • ATHENS • TOKYO • MILAN
MADRID • WARSAW • BUDAPEST • AUCKLAND

Recycling programs
for this product may
not exist in your area.

DOUBLE DECEPTION

A Worldwide Mystery/February 2011

First published by Thomas Bouregy & Co., Inc.

ISBN-13: 978-0-373-26741-5

Copyright © 2001 by Dorothy P. O'Neill

Printed in U.S.A.

To my daughter-in-law,
Catherine C. Barlow, M.D.,who helped me
in the medical areas of this book.
Thanks, Cathy.

PROLOGUE

IN THE SPACIOUS BEDROOM of his Fifth Avenue penthouse, Theodore Van Brunt Ormsby wakened and stretched his strong, muscular limbs for a few minutes amid the smooth-as-satin sheets. Though he'd retired long after midnight, he felt rested and full of energy. As he always did the morning after a late party, he congratulated himself for keeping his distance from alcohol.

A smug smile crossed his handsome, aristocratic face. He felt sure he was the only person at last night's bash without a hangover this morning. And that included Cherie. She'd had too much champagne and started hinting about marriage. He wasn't ready to break off with her yet, or he'd have done it right there at the party. Her spectacular blond-showgirl looks and dynamic personality had kept him from tiring of her. He still found her exciting. She'd lasted longer than any of the others.

A knock at the door roused him from his thoughts. Good old Judson had brought him the customary first cup of morning coffee. There was nothing like starting the day with the exotic flavor of one of his own custom blends. Throwing aside the brocade coverlet and reaching for the cashmere robe at the foot of his bed, he called, "Come in, Judson."

"Good morning, Mr. Ted. I trust you slept well."

"Very well, thank you, Judson."

They'd been exchanging these same greetings almost every morning for more than twelve years, but he and Judson went back much farther. He couldn't even remember when Judson hadn't been a servant in his parents' house.

Judson put the tray on the table near the window and opened the draperies. "It looks like a beastly day," he said. "It's starting to rain."

Ormsby looked out at the panoramic cityscape spreading beyond the penthouse. Rain or shine, he never tired of the view. "Well, this is typical March weather in New York," he said. "We should be glad it isn't snowing."

"Perhaps you should have stayed in Florida a fortnight or so longer, Mr. Ted," Judson replied.

He would have, if it hadn't been for Cherie's phone call saying her show was closing and she wanted to join him in Fort Lauderdale. It would have been a sticky situation if she'd found out he'd been doing the town every night with that model. But it was probably just as well he had left Florida when he did. He'd gotten in a little too deep with the model. Too late, he realized she believed everything he'd told her. She thought he was serious about her and actually wanted her to move to New York. Now, apparently, she was here in the city. According to Judson, she'd phoned him four times in the past ten days or so. Well, Judson would keep saying he was out of town. She'd get the idea and go back to Florida.

Watching Judson pour coffee from the sterling-silver pot into a fine china cup, he remembered this was Judson's day off. "Sorry it's such a rotten day for you," he said.

"It's quite all right, Mr. Ted. I shall be spending the time indoors at my sister's flat," Judson replied.

Ormsby remembered Judson hadn't been feeling up to par lately. Some sort of liver condition, according to Dr. Hammond. "Don't forget to take your medicine before you leave," he said. He didn't want anything to happen to Judson. He'd never get another houseman like him.

Judson smiled. "Thank you for reminding me, Mr. Ted. I shall take my daily dose straightaway, before I start preparing your breakfast."

As Ormsby showered and shaved in his profusely marbled and tiled bathroom, he turned his thoughts to the day ahead. Lunch at his club. A workout and a steam and rub in the afternoon. Theatre and supper with Cherie. His daily routine had fallen into the late-winter doldrums, he thought. But soon it would be time to spend more time at his Southhampton estate, have some weekend house parties, get in some tennis and golf and sailing. Even though Cherie wasn't into sports, he'd include her, of course—unless he'd grown tired of her by then.

After he dressed he went to the dining room. As usual, the *New York Times* lay at his place on the mahogany table next to a linen napkin.

Judson came out of the kitchen with a glass of freshly squeezed orange juice and a pot of coffee. "I'm preparing an omelet for you this morning, Mr. Ted," he said. "You haven't eaten eggs since Sunday last."

Ormsby enjoyed eating a substantial breakfast, but he was careful about his diet. He was determined not to die in middle age of a stroke or a heart attack as his father and grandfather had. But Dr. Hammond had assured him his cholesterol was low and he could eat eggs once or twice a week. "Fine, Judson. I'd enjoy an omelet today," he said.

He knew he was in excellent physical condition and he intended to stay that way. He couldn't understand how some men let themselves get out of shape. He knew even if he didn't have the physique of a Greek god, women would still be attracted to him because of his money. But it was satisfying to know that even if he were some poor working stiff, he had the looks to get any woman he wanted.

Judson's voice penetrated his thoughts. "Begging your pardon, Mr. Ted. I neglected to tell you that Miss Prentiss phoned again last night while you were out."

Ormsby frowned. *The model from Florida.* She was still in New York, still expecting to take up where they left off in Fort Lauderdale.

"Thank you, Judson. I assume you told her, again, that I was still out of town and you didn't know when I'd be back?"

"Yes, that's what I told her, Mr. Ted, but I'm not certain she believed me. She left her number again."

"And you're sure it's a Manhattan number?"

"Yes." Judson turned towards the kitchen door. "I'll see to your omelet now, Mr. Ted."

Ormsby scowled as he drank his orange juice. The model was getting to be a nuisance. Well, it was only a matter of time before she realized he wasn't interested in her anymore. He dismissed the matter from his mind and turned his attention to the newspaper.

After breakfast he took the newspaper to his study across the hall from the dining room. He was checking the financial pages when Judson appeared in the doorway.

"Unless there's something else I can do for you, Mr. Ted, I'll be leaving now," he said.

"No, nothing else. Run along, Judson, and enjoy your day. I'll see you in the morning."

He finished reading the paper and glanced at his watch. Time to turn on his computer and catch the opening stock-market figures. Just as he rose from his chair, the phone on his desk rang. It was probably Cherie wanting to know where they'd be having supper after the theatre tonight, he thought. He answered the phone. A moment later he cursed under his breath. *The Florida model.* With Judson not here to screen calls, he should have had sense enough to let it ring.

He listened to her half-angry, half-tearful questions. Why hadn't he returned her calls? Didn't he realize she'd moved to New York because of him? When was she going to see him?

Though he'd broken off with more women than he could remember, this would have to be handled differently, he decided. No final evening out, with all the trimmings. He decided to ask her to come to the penthouse this morning. They'd have coffee, and he'd explain to her that she'd mistaken their Florida fling for something permanent.

She agreed to come right away. Good, he thought, with a sigh of relief. The sooner he got this over with, the better. However, one detail bothered him. His success in parting amicably with women was in no small way due to the farewell gift bestowed on each one. A handsome piece of jewelry, often featuring her birthstone embellished with diamonds, had always taken the sting out of the brush-off. But in this case he'd had no time to shop for the parting gift. Suddenly he remembered the gold-and-pearl pendant he'd purchased for Cherie's birthday next week. He'd have plenty of time to get another one for Cherie.

He called the security guard in the lobby and told

him he was expecting a young lady very soon and he was to let her up on the private elevator without delay. Then he went to the kitchen and looked over the jars of his exotic blends of coffee beans. Though the kitchen was Judson's domain, Ormsby was expert at making coffee. He decided to brew something special for his visitor. It was the least he could do. They'd had a wonderful time together. Too bad she'd taken it seriously. Being rich and handsome sometimes had its drawbacks, he thought, with a rueful smile.

He ground the beans, savoring the aroma. There was nothing like his own special blends. How could people drink commercial coffees? They all tasted the same. When he experimented with his own blends, he never knew exactly how each one would taste. Rarely had any of them failed to please him.

Just as he finished brewing the coffee he heard the elevator doors open. There was no time to go to his bedroom and get the pendant. Well, after he broke the bad news, he'd tell her he had something for her and he'd go and get it.

A sense of unease came over him as he went into the foyer. He told himself to forget it. He'd done this dozens of times. There was no reason why this time should be any different.

She was standing near the elevator. He'd almost forgotten what a beauty she was. Too bad the timing was wrong. He wasn't ready to get rid of Cherie.

He put on his warm, engaging smile. He'd perfected it years ago, practicing in front of a mirror to get just the right touch of warmth in it. "We need to discuss what happened in Florida," he said. "Shall we talk about it over coffee?"

ONE

LIZ'S SENSES TINGLED with anticipation as Medical Examiner Dan Switzer drove the car along Fifth Avenue. Through the window, streaked with a mid-March rain, she could see they were almost there. In a few minutes she'd be at the scene of another homicide. This one promised to be one of the most interesting she'd ever followed. The murder victim was billionaire playboy Theodore Van Brunt Ormsby.

Some women were into gourmet cooking, quilting, or collecting Hummel figurines. Most everyone had some sort of consuming hobby. Hers was following murder cases and trying to figure out which suspect was guilty.

It started when she was a kid. Pop was a homicide detective. He encouraged her interest in murder cases and enjoyed answering her questions. "You'd make a first-rate detective, Lizzie," he often said.

Mom always looked worried when he said that. Liz knew she didn't want her only daughter following in Pop's footsteps. "One cop in the family is enough," she'd say. She'd been concerned when Sophie Pulaski applied to the Police Academy. Sophie was a cop now, temporarily assigned to Homicide Reports and Records.

Liz and Sophie had been inseparable friends since first grade at Our Lady Queen of Peace school on Staten Island. Sophie wanted to be a homicide detective. But Mom needn't worry about another Rooney on the force, Liz thought. Becoming a police detective didn't interest her; becoming a private investigator did. Someday, maybe she'd follow through on that.

Pop was retired from the force now, and he and Mom were having a great time travelling all around the country with their Taurus, hauling their mobile home. They'd left soon after her graduation from Wagner College last year. That could have been the end of her interest in murder cases. Without Pop's input, her hobby might have faded away. But thanks to Medical Examiner Dan Switzer, and Sophie's bits of information from Homicide, it had not only survived, but was stronger than ever.

She cast a fond look at Dan as he steered the car through the early-morning traffic. Dan and Pop had been friends for years. He'd known her since her pigtail days. To him, she'd always be Frank Rooney's red-haired, freckle-faced kid with a passion for solving murder mysteries, but that didn't keep him from offering her a job after she got out of college. The job itself entailed mostly computer work, but thanks to Dan it had one irresistible fringe benefit. Though she wasn't qualified to be on his forensic team, he took her along to homicide scenes whenever she chose to go.

She wouldn't have missed this one for anything. This was a rare case where she wouldn't feel sorry for the victim. Theodore Van Brunt Ormsby was a first-class cad. His habit of brushing off the old love and getting on with the new made the front pages of city tabloids regularly. Already she suspected that one of his cast-offs had killed him, and she could only feel he got what he deserved.

Dan's voice broke into her thoughts. "Here we are, Liz."

He pulled up and parked at the entrance to the tower of multimillion-dollar condominiums where Theodore Van Brunt Ormsby resided. The uniformed doorman standing under the green canopy put on a forbidding glare. Only the limousines of the tower's wealthy residents were allowed anywhere near the entrance, Liz decided. The doorman started to approach the car when he saw the official seal. He hastened to open the etched-glass doors leading into the elegantly furnished lobby.

"What's going on?" he asked Dan. "A bunch of cops went in a few minutes ago and now you. Something happen to one of the residents?"

"We're not sure yet," Dan replied.

Inside, the security guard was equally curious about the arrival of the medical examiner. "I just let some cops and some guys from your office up a few minutes ago," he said to Dan. He pushed the button to the private penthouse elevator. "What happened up there?"

Again, Dan replied, "We're not sure."

Actually, they were sure, Liz thought. According to Dan, Ormsby's physician had reported the death as a homicide.

She glanced at her watch. It was almost nine o'clock. Ormsby's murder would make the noontime TV news, and by late afternoon the tabloids would come out with glaring headlines and photos of him with his various romantic partners dating back to his college days. By evening, television's talking heads would deliver complete biographies with shots of him on the links of his private golf club, on the deck of his palatial yacht, and astride his favorite polo pony. And of course there would be shots of him with some of the women he'd cast aside. His current paramour would be included too. The media would have a field day.

When the elevator door opened onto a foyer crowded with gold-framed paintings and Persian rugs, an elderly gentleman greeted them, saying "I'm Dr. Hammond, Mr. Ormsby's physician. I assume you're the medical examiner."

"Yes, I'm Dr. Switzer," Dan replied. Liz suppressed a smile when he added, "And this is my assistant, Ms. Rooney." She was his assistant, all right, but not in the way Dan implied.

"Your forensic team is with the body, Dr. Switzer," the doctor said, as he led them along a hallway. "I'm sure you'll agree with me that Mr. Ormsby was poisoned. A police detective is here too, and the body has been photographed."

Liz hoped that George Eichle hadn't been put on the case. As he always did, he'd resent her presence at the scene. Eichle had made detective three years ago, before Pop retired. Pop liked him. "He's one of the brightest young cops I've seen in a long time," he told her. But there was nothing bright about the looks Eichle cast her way whenever he was at a murder scene and she showed up with Dan.

They followed Dr. Hammond past a gorgeously furnished living room the size of her entire apartment. It was bustling with cops checking for evidence. Considering Ormsby's reputation, they probably expected to find something like lipstick stains on a champagne goblet, a lone earring, or a stray article of feminine apparel.

The doctor led them into a bedroom dominated by an enormous bed with a tapestry spread and matching, fringed pillows scattered beneath its towering, walnut headboard. Either Mr. Ormsby had not gone to bed last night, or he'd risen early and a servant had already tended to making the bed, she thought.

"The body's in the bathroom," Dr. Hammond said, motioning towards a nearby door.

Just as he spoke, the rangy form of Detective Eichle appeared in the bathroom doorway. When he saw Liz he scowled. "You, again, Rooney?" he asked.

To counter the scowl she put on a smile. "Good morning to you too, Eichle," she said. Still scowling, he strode out of the bedroom.

"As I told Detective Eichle, I didn't disturb the body in any way," Dr. Hammond said to Dan. Liz followed Dan into a lavishly mirrored and marbled bathroom. There, the body of Theodore Van Brunt Ormsby sprawled, face up, on the floor. Except for the coat to match his finely tailored trousers, he was fully clothed. From newspaper photos she'd seen of him, she knew he'd been a good-looking man. His handsome features remained intact, but death had taken all expression from his face and eyes.

From a skylight, a shaft of sunshine played over the front of his custom-made shirt. A mess of dried vomit almost hid the monogram on the pocket. Considerable time must have passed since he'd thrown up, or the vomit wouldn't have had time to dry, she concluded. She wondered why the doctor was so sure he'd been poisoned. He could have taken ill, collapsed, and choked on his vomit. A moment later she rejected that idea. His mouth and chin showed only a minute trace of vomit. It looked as if the contents of his stomach had come to rest on his shirtfront. He must have thrown up before he collapsed.

As she continued to scrutinize the scene, she saw an open bottle of aspirin on the marble counter beside the washbasin, suggesting Ormsby had been stricken with a headache and come into the bathroom to take something for it. She noticed his suit coat slung over a chair. Maybe he'd started to undress for bed. It couldn't have been the other way around. He couldn't have been in the process of getting dressed for the day. It was common knowledge that Theodore Van Brunt Ormsby maintained his lavish lifestyle on sizeable fortunes inherited from parents and grandparents. He didn't need to get up early and go to work; he'd never worked a day in his life. This, plus the thought of the made-up bed, led her to believe he might have been getting ready to hit his fancy sack when the headache struck. Or had the headache struck earlier, perhaps while he was still out for the evening? She'd be better able to draw conclusions after the autopsy.

While Dan joined the forensic team in examining the body, she looked over her shoulder to make sure Eichle hadn't come back. Then she asked, "Who found the body, Dr. Hammond?"

"Judson, the houseman. He phoned me immediately. He didn't realize it was too late. He thought Mr. Ormsby was still alive and had suffered a heart attack."

Liz suppressed a smile. From what she'd heard about Theodore Van Brunt Ormsby, there was nothing wrong with his heart that a fling with a new Hollywood starlet, beauty-pageant winner, or cover-girl model wouldn't fix.

"I came right over, but when I got here I found he must have expired before Judson found him," the doctor continued. "Rigor mortis had started. Poor Judson—he was in the service of the Ormsby family while Ted was a child and came to work for him after Ted's parents died. He's devoted to him. He's all broken up about this."

Eichle was probably questioning Judson right now, Liz thought. She wished there were some way she could be in on the questioning, but she knew Eichle would never allow it. Dan looked up from the body. "He's been dead at least three hours," he said.

Ormsby must have been out on the town most of the night, Liz thought. Though his reputation as a playboy didn't include excessive drinking, he might have had a few too many. People did die from drinking too much alcohol in a short period of time. Alcohol poisoning. Was that what the doctor meant?

"Did Mr. Ormsby drink heavily?" she asked.

The doctor shook his head emphatically. "Absolutely not. He was close to being a total abstainer. He took only an occasional social glass."

"Sounds like you knew him very well."

"I did," the doctor replied. "Since he was a boy, in

fact. I've been the Ormsby family physician for many years." His face saddened. "Ted is—or was—the last of the Ormsbys. He was only thirty-eight."

Liz looked down at the body again. Dr. Hammond was convinced this was a homicide, but his close association with the Ormsby family could have turned his mind away from another possibility—suicide. The last of the Ormsbys might have deliberately poisoned himself. But why would a wealthy man in the prime of a life he obviously relished want to end it all? she asked herself. A possible answer flashed into her mind. Maybe he'd been diagnosed with a terminal illness. "How was his health?" she asked.

"Excellent. He was somewhat of a fitness buff. He worked out regularly at his club, and played golf and enjoyed polo and sailing at his place in the Hamptons. He watched his diet and didn't smoke or use recreational drugs. If you looked into his medicine cabinet you wouldn't find anything there except some over-the-counter product for an occasional headache, and as I've already told you, he was an extremely moderate social drinker. I gave him his annual physical examination less than two months ago and everything checked out one hundred percent."

Apparently Theodore Van Brunt Ormsby's only weakness was women, Liz thought.

"Every physician knows in rare instances heart attacks do occur no matter what recent tests show," the doctor said. "I might have thought this was one of those cases if he hadn't vomited, probably several hours ago."

What a shock this must have been for the house-man, Liz thought. Maybe she could find him and talk to him. "Where would I find Judson?" she asked the doctor.

"He was sitting in the hallway with one of the cops while his quarters and the kitchen were being searched for evidence," Dr. Hammond replied.

She walked down a hallway leading to the kitchen. As she approached it, a police officer came out, carrying a paper bag. A moment later, she saw Eichle in the hall talking to another man.

"I need to ask you a few questions, Mr. Judson," she heard Eichle say. "The evidence has been collected from the kitchen, so we can go in there." After they went into the kitchen, she tiptoed to the doorway and stole a look inside. Eichle was standing with his back to the doorway. Judson was facing it.

A slightly built man somewhere in his late sixties, Judson's face showed the strain of severe shock. She heard him ask Eichle if he'd like coffee during the questioning. He'd just ground some beans before the police came, he said. Liz noticed he spoke with a British accent.

Eichle nodded. "Sure. Thanks." He sat down at the table.

Liz watched Judson prepare a tray with coffee service and take it to the table. China cups and saucers, silver spoons, fine linen. This was as close as Eichle would get to a billionaire's lifestyle, she thought with a wry smile.

As Judson poured the steaming liquid into Eichle's cup, a wonderful aroma wafted out to the hall where she was lurking. She watched Eichle raise his cup for his first quaff and heard the pleased note in his voice. "Say—this is great coffee."

Judson gave a sad smile. "It's one of Mr. Ted's favorite blends. He liked his coffees, Mr. Ted did. You might say it was a hobby of his, collecting all different kinds of beans. Some he got in his travels and some he got imported. He enjoyed experimenting with them to get unusual flavors. He kept a record of how he blended them—like a recipe book you might say. The blend you're drinking is from several places in South America."

Someone with access to this kitchen could have slipped betel nuts or some other poisonous beans into Ormsby's collection, Liz thought. Though she disliked the thought, Judson could have done this more easily than anyone.

"I understand you're the one who found the body," she heard Eichle say.

"Yes, Officer, I did, only I didn't know he was dead. I thought he'd been taken ill."

"What time did you find him?"

"It was half after seven this morning. I took his coffee to his bedroom as usual, but he wasn't there, and I saw his bed hadn't been slept in. I thought this quite unusual because he hadn't told me he was to be gone overnight. He always lets me know when he plans to be out all night. Then I noticed the bathroom door was open and the light was on." Judson's eyes reddened. "That's when I found him."

"What did you do then?"

"I picked up Mr. Ted's cell phone and rang Dr. Hammond."

"The cell phone was in the bathroom?"

"Yes. It was lying on the floor beside him. I thought he must have felt ill and tried to ring the doctor."

"Where's the cell phone now?"

"I put it on the dresser in his bedroom."

Ormsby had realized he needed medical attention, Liz decided. He'd either passed out or died before he could place the call.

Unless someone had taken the phone away from him while he was trying to punch the number.

Eichle must have had a similar thought. "When did you last see Mr. Ormsby alive?" she heard him ask.

"Yesterday morning, just before I went off for the day. I always go to my sister's in Brooklyn on my free day. I leave immediately after breakfast and return the following morning in time to serve Mr. Ted his first cup of coffee. He always took it in his bedroom while I prepared his breakfast."

"So, when you came back this morning, you expected he'd be in his bedroom?"

"Yes, Officer. Like I said, he always lets me know if he's to be gone overnight."

"Was he also in the habit of letting you know his daily plans?"

"Yes, Officer, he always did that too."

"What did he tell you about his plans for yesterday and last evening?"

"He said he was lunching at his club and he was going to the theatre in the evening and for supper afterwards."

"I assume he wasn't going out for the evening alone."

Judson gave a faint smile. "When Mr. Ted went out evenings he always had a young lady with him."

"Did he mention the name of the young lady he was going out with last night?"

"I knew it was Miss Cherie La Salle. She's a new lady he's been seeing for several weeks."

Cherchez la femme. The old murder-mystery cliché was highly appropriate in the case of this womanizing playboy, Liz thought. *Look for the woman.* Miss Cherie La Salle would be the first woman Eichle questioned.

Her imagination sprang into action. Suppose Ormsby had told this Cherie woman he was ending their relationship and last night was to be their final evening together. True to the stereotype of the woman scorned, she'd planned revenge. After the theatre, in some dimly lit Manhattan supper club, she'd laced his coffee with a potent poison. He was so accustomed to exotic-tasting coffees, he didn't even notice. But whatever she used, it had to be slow acting. Otherwise he would have died right there in the supper club. Eichle's voice penetrated her thoughts. "Well, that does it, Judson. Thanks for your cooperation."

Just as she heard the scrape of his chair, footsteps sounded in the hall, and Dr. Hammond appeared. "They're getting ready to remove the body," he said, joining her outside the kitchen door. "We'll soon know what kind of poison it was."

Judson looked up at the sound of his voice. Eichle turned around. Liz didn't have time to duck out of sight.

"May I serve you coffee, Doctor? Miss?" Judson asked.

The doctor shook his head. "No, thank you, Judson." He looked at Liz, adding, "I can't stomach any of Ted's fancy blends. I like my coffee plain."

"I'd like some, Judson," Liz said. She ignored Eichle's dour glance and sat down at the table, saying, "I'm Liz Rooney. I'm with the medical examiner." Eichle left the kitchen a moment later, muttering something about checking to see what the cops had found in their search of the premises.

"Well, I must leave," Dr. Hammond said. "The medical examiner said he'd let me know the results of the autopsy. I'd appreciate it if you'd remind him. Judson will give you my office number and my home number too, in case you can't reach me at the office."

Judson, filling Liz's cup, watched him go. With a shake of his head, he said, "The doctor told me he believes someone poisoned Mr. Ted."

"But you don't believe that?" Liz asked.

"No. I can't think of anyone who'd do such a thing."

"How about one of the women in Mr. Ormsby's past?"

Judson looked uncomfortable, as if he were unwilling to acknowledge his employer's penchant for short-lived relationships. She was sure he was aware of the code his Mr. Ted lived by. Off with the old love and on with the new and variety is the spice of life. He'd probably been watching women come and go since Ormsby's college days.

"It's true Mr. Ted had a succession of lady friends," Judson admitted. "But none of them held any animosity after the relationships were terminated. He always gave them handsome parting gifts."

Dumped with diamonds, Liz thought, with a wry smile. She sipped her coffee. Eichle was right. It was good. "Delicious coffee, Judson," she said.

"It's one of Mr. Ted's favorites," he replied.

Just then she noticed a bottle of prescription medicine on the table. *Charles Judson,* the label read.

The instructions were printed too small for her to read without Judson noticing, but she was able to catch the name of the prescribing physician. It was Dr. Hammond. Poor old Judson, she thought. Not only did he have some sort of illness, but now he was without employment or a place to live.

At that moment, Dan stuck his head in the door. "We're ready to go, Liz," he said.

Liz rose from her chair, saying, "Thanks for the coffee, Judson."

"My pleasure, Madam," he replied.

Once in the hallway, she noticed the cops had finished in the living room. She glanced down the corridor towards the bedroom. Dan noticed and shook his head in mock exasperation. "Okay." He smiled. "I'll wait a few minutes while you go and see what they've found."

As she approached the bedroom, she heard Eichle's voice. "Did you check the answering machine for messages?" She listened outside the door. A few moments later she heard a recording: *"Seven-ten a.m. You have one message."* Her senses went on alert. She stood still a few feet away from the door and waited.

A woman's voice came on. "Forgive me for calling you so early, darling, but I just had to find out how you're feeling." A slight pause followed. "Why aren't you picking up, Ted? If you were sick enough to cancel our theatre date last night I know you're there." Another pause, and then, "Well, maybe you're in the bathroom. I hope you're not getting the flu or something. I can't imagine you being sick; you're always so healthy. You probably need to rest so I won't phone again. Call me when you feel up to it. Bye, darling."

The caller was undoubtedly the current paramour, Cherie La Salle, Liz decided, and it sounded as if she had an alibi. But, what if she'd deliberately staged the phone call to make it seem as if she hadn't seen Ormsby last night?

She felt certain Eichle had picked up on that possibility. No doubt he'd already found out a lot of things about this case while she could only guess. But at least she'd know before he did what kind of poison had killed Ormsby. With a smile of satisfaction she went to join Dan at the elevator.

TWO

BY THE TIME THEY REACHED the lobby, a small crowd had gathered outside the building. The arrival of an ambulance and the appearance of the shrouded body on the gurney had created the usual morbid curiosity. Police had erected barriers to keep onlookers at bay, and the doorman and security guard were trying to placate residents of the building who'd come down to the lobby, unaware of the situation.

The instant they got off the elevator, the security guard hurried towards them. "Was that Mr. Ormsby they took away?" he asked.

Dan nodded. The guard shook his head and sighed. "With all the cops going up there and then you, I knew something bad had happened."

At that moment a cop approached Dan saying he wanted to have a word with him. Dan told Liz he'd meet her at the car in a few minutes.

While Dan talked to the cop, she'd have time to question the security guard, Liz decided. Eichle was still in the penthouse. Evidently he hadn't questioned the guard yet. The ID badge on the guard's uniform read *C. W. Bowes.* She remembered Pop saying it never hurt to be kind when questioning a possible witness. "I know this is a shock for you, Mr. Bowes," she said. "Do you feel up to answering some questions?"

"Sure, Officer." He motioned towards his desk in an alcove across the lobby.

He thought she was a cop! If she told him she wasn't, he might not give her any information. Her moment of indecision was fleeting. She pulled a notebook and pencil out of her purse and followed him to his desk.

"When did you last see Mr. Ormsby?" she asked.

"Yesterday about twelve-thirty," he replied. "I guess he was on his way out for lunch. Judson— he's the houseman—he was off yesterday. I seen him leave about quarter past nine."

Liz pondered this for a moment. "What time did Mr. Ormsby return?"

"I didn't see him come back. It must have been after four o'clock. That's when I go off duty. The man on the next shift would know."

She wished there were some way she could question the other guard. But at least she could get as much information as possible from Mr. Bowes before Eichle came down from the penthouse. "Did Mr. Ormsby have any visitors after Judson left?" she asked.

Her heart leapt when the guard nodded emphatically. "Yes. A young lady went up to the penthouse at quarter of ten."

Liz's senses tingled. This woman couldn't have gotten past the guard without identifying herself and being announced. "I assume she gave you her name and you phoned Mr. Ormsby," she said.

Bowes shook his head. "I didn't ask for her name because Mr. Ormsby called down and said he was expecting a lady in a few minutes and I was to let her up right away. He didn't give me her name, and when she came in I didn't ask. With him expecting her I didn't think I had to."

Some of Liz's excitement ebbed. She'd been hoping to get a name, but just knowing about the woman visitor was a lot better than nothing. "How long did she stay up there?" she asked.

As if to compensate for not getting the young woman's name, Mr. Bowes hastened to say he'd written down the times of her arrival and departure. "She came down exactly twenty-six minutes after she went up," he said.

"Can you describe this woman?"

The suggestion of a grin penetrated the guard's face. "Sure. She was a real looker. Young—early twenties I'd say. Long dark hair. And she was tall."

This willowy, dark-haired beauty fit right into Ormsby's big parade of rejects, Liz thought. "I take it you'd never seen this woman before," she said.

"Never laid eyes on her till she showed up yesterday. But, like I said, I go off duty at four. One of the night men might have seen her, but…" He paused.

"But what?" Liz asked.

"I always look at the night logs when I get here in the morning, and I can tell you Mr. Ormsby wasn't one for having women visit him alone. When he had company, it was always parties with men and women both."

Ormsby's ties with his women were loose, but part of him was as straitlaced as a Victorian corset, Liz thought. No hanky panky in his penthouse. Why, then, had he welcomed this beautiful brunet after Judson left?

"Let's go, Liz." Dan's voice broke into her musing.

Her speculation continued on the drive back to the office. There were now three real suspects, she decided—Judson, Cherie La Salle, and this beautiful visitor. Of the three, Judson was the only one for whom she couldn't figure a motive. When Dan phoned Homicide with the results of the autopsy, maybe Eichle would divulge some information; or if Eichle attended the autopsy, maybe he'd tell Dan something. She decided this was unlikely. Eichle wouldn't tell Dan anything. He wouldn't risk Dan passing the information on to her.

But for the past few months she'd had an extra source of information—her best friend, Sophie. She was in the same precinct as Eichle, temporarily assigned to clerical work in Homicide. Knowing Liz's passion for solving murder cases, she kept her ears open. Perhaps Sophie would have something interesting to report today.

SHE'D BEEN BACK at her desk for about an hour when Sophie phoned. "Homicide's all stirred up about the playboy poisoning," she said. "Did you get to the scene?"

"You know I wouldn't have passed this one up," Liz replied. "It was worth being glared at by Eichle. Has he come back yet? Did you pick up on anything?"

"Only that Sid Rothman's been put on the case with him."

Rothman and Eichle made an efficient though physically mismatched team, Liz thought. Rothman was short, pudgy, and balding, with a round, perpetually affable face. Eichle was lean and lanky with shaggy brown hair, craggy features, and a no-nonsense look about him. An ideal combo for a good-cop–bad-cop routine.

"I heard them talking about working together on the case," Sophie said.

Sophie had become quite adept at overhearing discussions among the homicide detectives. She said it was good experience while she was waiting to be eligible for homicide-detective training. With Sophie a homicide detective, following murder cases would be a breeze, Liz thought with a smile.

"Let's meet after work and I'll fill you in on whatever else I might pick up," Sophie said.

"Okay. See you at the newsstand, as usual."

"Good," Sophie said. "We can go for coffee at that place around the corner and talk. I'm meeting Ralph later, so I can't stay long. You seeing Wade tonight?"

"Unfortunately, yes."

They both laughed. Sophie knew all about the hassle with Wade. Liz had met him through Dan and his wife. He was nice-looking, a Wall Street stockbroker who lived in the same apartment building as the Switzers. "A very eligible bachelor," Dan's wife, Edna, had said when she set up the blind date.

Liz had liked him a lot at first. During the first few weeks of seeing one another, her interest in murder cases seemed to amuse him, but lately he'd been saying it was an obsession and she should knock it off. Lucky she wasn't in love with him. His attitude had ruined everything.

"Maybe he'll lighten up," Sophie said. She'd met Wade a couple of weeks ago when she and her boyfriend, Ralph Perillo, had gone to dinner with Liz and Wade. Ralph was a cop too, assigned to another precinct. They'd met in Police Academy.

Liz shook her head. "I don't think he's going to lighten up. I'm almost ready to dump him."

"If you do, Ralph and I will find you a nice cop," Sophie said with a laugh.

JUST BEFORE SHE WENT OUT for lunch, Liz turned on the TV in her office. Ormsby's murder had made the noontime news. There wasn't anything there that she didn't already know, she thought. In fact, she knew more about the case than the newscaster. The thought made her smile.

LATE THAT AFTERNOON Dan came to her desk. "Ormsby's death was caused by an overdose of chlorotriazide," he said.

Liz reached for her notebook. "What's chloro-whatever-you-said and how do you spell it?"

Dan laughed. "It's a drug used in prescription medicines." He spelled it for her, adding, "It's commonly known as Lasix—generally prescribed for kidney and liver problems. The autopsy showed a substantial amount of it in Ormsby's system. It was ingested with coffee."

The first thing Liz thought of was Judson's medicine. Did it contain Lasix? Even if it did, what was Judson's motive? She hated to think he might have put some of it in Ormsby's morning coffee. She remembered the bottle was large. She hadn't noticed how much medicine it contained, but she felt sure it hadn't been empty this morning. "What would be a substantial amount?" she asked.

"It's difficult to say, exactly. Lasix is highly toxic if it isn't carefully monitored. And apparently he'd taken aspirin later, which only made things worse."

Liz pondered this. How could Judson have poisoned Ormsby's morning coffee when the guard saw Ormsby leave the building at half past twelve? "How long does it take for this medicine to kill someone?" she asked, hoping he'd say an overdose would result in a speedy death. That would let Judson off the hook.

"Lasix is a slow-acting drug," Dan replied. "Depending on the victim's physical condition and the quantity ingested, the first reaction would be felt anywhere from one to eight hours, but death wouldn't necessarily come till much later."

Dan went back to his office, and, with a sinking heart, Liz had to admit Judson could have done it. He could have added the drug to the second cup of coffee Ormsby drank at breakfast. She mulled it over in her mind. Ormsby had been able to pursue whatever activities he'd scheduled for that afternoon. It wasn't until he returned to the penthouse that he began to feel ill. That's when he cancelled the theatre date with Cherie. But two factors kept her from thinking of Judson as the most likely suspect. She didn't know for sure if his medicine was Lasix, and as far as she knew, he didn't have a motive.

As for Ormsby's beautiful brunet visitor, if she was, indeed, one of his cast-offs, she not only had a motive for killing him, but the opportunity as well. The entire scene played out in her mind. The willowy beauty had gone to Ormsby's penthouse that morning to try and revive their relationship. They'd had coffee in the kitchen while they discussed it. When he made it clear the relationship was definitely over, she poured some of Judson's medicine into Ormsby's cup when he wasn't looking. Maybe he'd left the table to get the sugar bowl or something, and she'd seized the opportunity.

The beautiful brunet visitor was a prime suspect, Liz decided. But she hadn't forgotten Cherie La Salle's early-morning phone call and the suspicion that it had been staged. Maybe Ormsby hadn't cancelled the date at all. Maybe he'd dumped her during supper that evening, and after he told her the bad news she'd poured Lasix into his coffee while he was in the men's room. To divert suspicion from herself, she'd faked the phone call. The trouble with that idea was why she would be carrying around a bottle of Lasix in her evening bag. Somehow the idea of Cherie having liver or kidney problems seemed highly unlikely.

She knew she was casting at straws, hoping Judson was not the guilty one.

SOPHIE WAS WAITING for her at the newsstand.

"Look," she said, thrusting a tabloid at her. "Your poisoned playboy's all over the front page."

Liz surveyed the glaring headline. Billionaire Playboy Bumped Off. She studied the photo of Ormsby shown alighting from a limo with a beautiful, shapely blonde. She read the text below. *Theodore Van Brunt Ormsby arriving at a recent charity event with Broadway showgirl Cherie La Salle.*

"There's more on the inside pages," Sophie said. "You can read it while we're having our coffee."

In the coffee shop, Liz read the rest of the coverage. Photographs of Ormsby engaging in his favorite pursuits—yachting, polo, and women—took up most of the first two inside pages, interspersed with more copy. A brief biography was featured, along with quotations from various friends and associates. The text also stated that Cherie La Salle was in seclusion and could not be reached for comments.

"This doesn't mention suspects," Liz said.

"I guess the paper went to press before the police had much to go on," Sophie replied. "Maybe there'll be more on the evening TV news."

"Did you overhear anything after you phoned me?" Liz asked.

"Yes. Eichle interviewed Ormsby's attorney. I know who's getting his money."

"Great! So who hit the jackpot?"

"Ormsby's butler, or whatever you call the man who works in his penthouse; he came into a neat little bundle, and his doctor got something too, and some servants on his estate in Southhampton. The rest went to his prep school and college and his church and various charities."

Judson, Liz thought, with a sinking heart. This

could have been his motive. But she still couldn't bring herself to believe he'd poisoned the young man to whom he'd been so devoted. However, money was a powerful force. If Ormsby had told him about the sizeable legacy, he might have been influenced. Maybe he needed money for his sister in Brooklyn who had to have life-saving surgery, or maybe he'd done some gambling and was now in the clutches of unscrupulous loan sharks. But even if either far-fetched situation were true, surely Ormsby would have given him the money if he knew.

"What do you think?" Sophie asked. "Did the butler do it? Or the doctor?"

Liz hadn't considered Dr. Hammond a suspect, but now she knew he had the same motive as Judson. As a physician he might have had the opportunity. If this Lasix stuff came in tablets as well as liquid, he could have ground them up and slipped some into Ormsby's sugar bowl.

"I suppose either one of them could have done it," she said. "But I haven't ruled out Cherie La Salle. Did you hear anything about any money being left to her?"

Sophie shook her head. "According to what I over-heard, the only woman who got anything was the housekeeper on his Southampton estate."

Poor timing for Cherie, Liz thought. In a few more weeks she'd probably have been the recipient of one of those handsome parting gifts Judson had mentioned.

She thought again of the beautiful brunet visitor. "Did you overhear any talk about a woman who came to Ormsby's penthouse the morning before he was found dead?" she asked.

"No, but they might have talked about it when I was on my break."

"Well, keep your ears open tomorrow—okay?"

"Sure." Sophie's eyes sparkled. "This is fun. I'm getting almost as good at it as you."

"Maybe someday we can set up our own private investigating firm," Liz said with a laugh.

Sophie laughed too. "Rooney and Pulaski, Private Eyes. It has a nice ring to it."

"Meanwhile, let's concentrate on deciding who poisoned Ormsby before Eichle does," Liz said.

"You'd really like to stick it to him, wouldn't you?"

Liz nodded. She imagined herself jotting down a name in her notebook and underlining it. This would be the name of her person she believed to be guilty. She would put a date next to it to remind herself just when she'd made her decision. It would be a way of matching wits with the homicide detective— especially Eichle. She knew her chances were slim of outwitting him. He had access to Ormsby's ad- dress book, to telephone-company records, and other information which could wind up as hard evidence.

That's what made this so challenging. If the name she
wrote down turned out to be the same as the person
convicted for this crime, she'd feel as if she'd won.

They finished their coffee and prepared to leave—
Sophie to meet Ralph, Liz to head home and wait for
Wade to come and take her out for dinner. Since Mom
and Pop had sold the house on Staten Island, home
had been a studio apartment near Gramercy park.
They'd given her whatever furnishings she wanted.
Most everything else they sold or gave away. When
they finally got around to buying their retirement
home they wanted everything new. Though the apartment was small, it had a view of the park. She liked
it.

Sophie still lived with her parents on Staten Island.
They'd talked about renting a larger apartment, together, but that was before Ralph came into the picture. There'd been no talk of it lately. Liz suspected
Sophie and Ralph were getting serious.

As she walked from the subway to her apartment
building, she hoped Wade wouldn't give her a hard
time again tonight about her interest in murder cases.
She hadn't been kidding when she told Sophie she
was ready to dump him if he didn't lighten up. She
had a feeling there'd be a showdown tonight.

HER INSTINCTS WERE RIGHT. She sensed trouble the
instant Wade arrived at her apartment.

"Well, I suppose this was a red-letter day for you," he said.

"I guess you're talking about the playboy poisoning," she replied.

"What else?" he retorted. "When I heard about it I knew you'd be right there at the murder scene, getting in on all the gory details and loving every minute of it."

"Why does that bother you so much?" she asked.

"Because it's not normal for someone to be obsessed with murders, especially a woman. It's very unfeminine."

Her anger began to rise. "This is a great way to start the evening. Are you going to harass me all through dinner?"

"Maybe I should. Maybe then you'd come to your senses."

"Don't hold your breath," she said.

He cast her a dark look. "I've been hoping you'd get over this morbid interest before my mother comes to visit me. I wanted her to meet you, but if you let it slip that you're into murders she'd never approve of you."

In preparation for going out, she'd picked up her purse and slung a coat over her shoulders. Now she tossed both onto the couch, saying, "We'd better call this off, Wade."

He looked at her in surprise. "Cancel our dinner date?"

"Not just our dinner...*us,*" she said. "It's clear you're not willing to accept me as I am, and I'm not making myself over for you and your mother."

He glared at her for a moment. "Call me when you've reconsidered," he said. Without another word or glance, he turned and left, giving the door a deliberate slam.

She knew he was arrogant enough to believe she didn't mean what she'd said, but it would be a hot day at the North Pole before she'd ever call him. As far as she was concerned, it was over.

THREE

SHE WAKENED THE NEXT morning with a sense of relief. Till now she hadn't realized how stifling her relationship with Wade had become. For more than a month she'd been unable to talk freely about the interest she found so challenging.

What a bad situation it would have been if she'd fallen in love with him. She pictured herself being presented to Wade's mother. If Mama were anything like Son, she'd be good-looking, mildly arrogant, and reeking with aristocratic culture.

After a quiz about family background, Mama would have delved into personal matters. "What do you enjoy in your leisure time, Elizabeth?" she'd ask. "Do you collect dolls or do needlepoint?" With a warning glance from Wade she'd find herself barely able to speak, lest she blurt out the awful truth.

SHE'D BEEN AT HER DESK only a few minutes when Dan came in. "You want to go down to the morgue with me, Liz?" he asked. "Eichle's bringing in a young woman for possible identification of her missing sister. He thinks there's a connection to the Ormsby case."

Liz felt a twinge of excitement. "Did he say why he thinks there's a connection?"

"No. He only said she was hysterical when she came into the squad room. She said her sister had been depressed and she was afraid she might have committed suicide. That's why I want to go down to the morgue. If it turns out it's her sister she'll need some comforting."

Dan had a kind heart, Liz thought. He figured Eichle wouldn't be any good at comforting. When it came to investigation Eichle was tops, but she couldn't imagine him offering his shoulder for anyone to cry on.

How did Eichle figure a connection between this woman and Ormsby's murder? she asked herself. The answer came in a flash. Eichle suspected this missing sister was the young woman who'd visited Ormsby in his penthouse yesterday. He'd probably called the guard to come to the morgue too. If the sister and the guard both identified the body, that meant the missing sister and the beautiful brunet were one and the same. Throw in a motive and the case was as good as solved.

Figuring a motive was easy. The missing sister was one of Ormsby's rejects, perhaps the one who'd preceded Cherie La Salle. She must have phoned him yesterday morning after Judson left, saying she needed to talk to him. Since he always remained on good terms with his ex-flames, he agreed, and told the guard he was expecting a lady and it was okay to let her on the elevator right away.

The scene unfolded in Liz's mind. Whether Judson had brewed fresh coffee before he left, or whether Ormsby had brewed it himself, he and the brunet beauty had gone into the kitchen and talked while drinking one of Ormsby's exotic blends. The bottle containing Judson's medicine was on the table.

The rest Liz had already established. The woman had come to the penthouse hoping to rekindle the romance. When Ormsby told her it was definitely over, she found the right moment to pour some of Judson's medicine into his cup.

Maybe she hadn't intended to kill him. Maybe she only wanted to make him sick. Then, the next day, she learned he was dead. Overcome with grief and remorse, she'd thrown herself into the Hudson River or perhaps the East River, or jumped off the Empire State Building, or…

WHEN SHE AND DAN got to the viewing area, Eichle was already there with the young woman whose sister was missing. The woman's back was turned. She was looking through the glass where an attendant had just wheeled a shrouded body.

Eichle scowled when he saw Liz. She ignored the scowl. "Hello, Eichle," she said.

At the sound of her voice the woman turned around. Liz was startled to find herself looking into the most beautiful face she'd ever seen. Blue-violet eyes, dark hair cascading to her shoulders, and a willowy yet curvaceous shape completed the picture. Even more startling was her realization that this gorgeous creature fit the security guard's description of Ormsby's mysterious visitor perfectly.

Through her surprise she heard Dan's kind voice. "I'm Dr. Switzer, the medical examiner. Detective Eichle brought you here because the vital statistics of this body match those of your missing sister."

"My name is Heather," the young woman said. "Heather Prentiss." She glanced through the glass at the shrouded body. Her voice quivered. "That body couldn't possibly be my sister. I know she's alive, somewhere."

Liz stared at her in puzzlement. Dan had told her the woman had been hysterical when she came into Homicide and said her sister had been depressed.

"You reported her as missing and a possible suicide," Eichle said.

The young woman nodded. "I know, but I was terribly upset when Clover didn't come home last night and I didn't hear from her, and I guess I let my imagination run away with me. I'm sorry you had to bring me here for nothing."

How could she be sure it was for nothing if her sister was depressed? Liz wondered.

Dan must have had the same thought. "Let's make

certain," he said. He signaled the attendant, who un-covered the face.

The young woman barely glanced at it. "That's not my sister," she said, with a shake of her head. "I knew it wasn't. Clover probably came home after I left this morning. She's probably waiting for me, wondering where I am."

"I can see she's not your sister," Eichle said. "She doesn't look anything like you. Well, thanks, Miss Prentiss. We'll call you if we need you to come in again."

"I know Clover's not dead," the young woman said, as she left.

Liz wondered why Eichle had remarked about the lack of resemblance. She couldn't hold back a com-ment. "Many sisters don't look alike, Eichle."

"In this instance they do," he snapped. "They're identical twins—not that it's any of your business."

Liz wasn't sure which surprised her more—the fact that the two sisters were identical twins, or that Eichle had revealed this information to her. She sensed he didn't want this information known. In the heat of his anger with her he'd let it slip. The expression on his face confirmed this. He looked as if he wanted to kick himself.

Just then the door opened. Mr. Bowes, the security guard, came in. Liz noticed a puzzled frown on his face as he approached Eichle. "You said you needed me to identify the body of a missing woman," he said. "You thought it might be the woman I saw go up to Mr. Ormsby's penthouse the day before he was found dead. Well, I don't have to look; it ain't her." He jerked his thumb in the direction of the door. "That woman who came out of here just now—she's the one I seen go up to the penthouse."

Just then he noticed Liz. He smiled in recognition, saying, "Hello, Officer." Liz knew Eichle was now aware she'd talked to the guard before he did. This could only add to his ire. Also, he wouldn't like her being addressed as a police officer.

Eichle cast her a baleful glance before addressing Mr. Bowes. "The woman you saw in the hall is the missing woman's sister. She says there's a strong resemblance. That's why you mistook her for the woman you saw go up to the penthouse."

Again, Liz thought Eichle didn't want it known that the sisters were identical twins. For some reason, he wanted this kept under wraps.

"The woman you saw in the corridor has already stated that this body is not her sister," Eichle said. "Will you have a look and tell me if she's the one you saw go up to the penthouse yesterday?"

Mr. Bowes stepped up to the glass. He shook his head. "No, that's not her." He left, looking bewildered.

Suddenly Liz remembered an old Bette Davis movie she'd seen a long time ago on TV. In it, one twin had died. Had the other twin murdered her?

She couldn't remember. But she did recall one twin had assumed the other's identity. Had Eichle seen the movie, and the idea of a switched identity occurred to him? Was that why he wanted to keep the twin factor out of the headlines?

Apparently, the missing twin was his prime suspect. Heather must have told him plenty about her twin. She wished she knew what it was. She hoped Sophie had kept her ears open this morning.

Sophie phoned her later in the day. "I didn't get a chance to call earlier," she said. "Can you meet me after work or do you have something on with Wade?"

"Wade and I broke up last night," Liz replied.

"You really dumped him?"

"Well, it was more or less a mutual decision. I'll tell you all about it tonight."

LIZ GOT TO THE NEWSSTAND first. While waiting, she bought a tabloid. Again, Ormsby's murder dominated the front page and the first two inside pages. She scanned the photos and text. The only new development was a statement from the police department. A search was on for a woman who'd visited Ormsby in his penthouse the morning before he was found dead. The woman's sister had reported her missing and a possible suicide. The missing woman was described as a slender, white female about twenty years old with dark hair. Neither her name nor her sister's was given and no mention was made that the sisters were twins.

The police were protecting the identity and privacy of the other twin, Heather, Liz decided. She'd be hounded by news media if word got out she was the twin sister of a suspect in Ormsby's murder. No wonder Eichle was annoyed when Dan brought her to the morgue this morning. She wished she could convince him she knew when to keep her mouth shut. The only person she'd discussed the case with was Sophie, and Sophie was privy to the information anyway.

Sophie arrived. "I have something to tell you," she said, as they walked to the coffeehouse. "A really gorgeous gal came into the station this morning to report her sister missing since yesterday. The cop on the desk was going to send her to Missing Persons but she got hysterical and said her sister was in a deep depression and might have committed suicide, so she was sent up to Homicide. Eichle and Rothman talked with her but I couldn't hear everything they said. After they'd talked awhile, Eichle left the building with this woman. I thought I heard him tell Rothman they were going to the morgue."

"For once I'm ahead of you," Liz said with a laugh. She showed Sophie the police statement in the evening newspaper and told her what happened at the morgue.

"You found out more than I did this morning," Sophie said. "Identical twins! Heather and Clover. Their mother must have been into wildflowers. But how do you suppose Eichle and Rothman made a connection between this Heather and the woman seen going to Ormsby's penthouse?"

"Her looks. They probably picked up on it when she told them she and her missing sister were identical twins. I'm sure the security guard didn't leave anything out when he described the gorgeous woman who went up to the penthouse."

"She's fantastic-looking, all right," Sophie said. "Every guy in the squad room was drooling."

When they settled themselves in the coffeehouse, Liz said, "Tell me what you make of this. In the morgue this morning Heather hardly even looked at the body because she insisted her sister was alive."

"What!" Sophie looked her in disbelief. "That's a real switch. At the station a few minutes earlier, she thought her sister had killed herself. I don't know what to think."

"It reminds me of that old Bette Davis movie we saw," Liz said.

"The one where one twin sister died and the other one assumed her identity. You don't think Heather's pulling something like that, do you?"

"No. The circumstances are different, but the missing-twin thing made me think of the movie."

"Clover could have poisoned Ormsby and then

killed Heather and gotten rid of her body and gone to the police pretending to be Heather and reported her missing saying she was depressed and probably killed herself," Sophie said.

Liz laughed. "Your imagination is even wilder than mine."

"Just kidding," Sophie said. "Heather was very upset when she came into the station. I got the feeling she and Clover are very close. I don't see how she could have faked those tears."

"They must be very close, but how come Heather suddenly decided that Clover is alive?"

"You got me," Sophie replied. "But I think Clover must have poisoned Ormsby and then committed suicide."

"I agree that Clover poisoned him, but I'm not sure she committed suicide. She could be alive somewhere, in hiding or on the run."

"Well, one thing's certain," Sophie said. "Eichle and Rothman can't get anywhere with this case till they find Clover, dead or alive."

Liz sighed. "I wish I knew more about Clover. I'd like to find out if she was really depressed when she disappeared." Heather must have told Eichle and Rothman something to have them chalk Clover up as their prime suspect, she thought. If only she could find out what they knew.

Suddenly Sophie straightened up in her chair. A look of excitement lit her face. "She's here," she whispered. "*Heather*. She's over there near the window."

Liz followed her excited stare. Sure enough, she saw Heather Prentiss alone at a table across the room. This was her chance to find out more about Clover, she thought. "I'm going over there," she said.

Sophie looked at her watch. "I'm meeting Ralph at the movie theatre in a few minutes anyway. Good luck!"

FOUR

LIZ WALKED OVER to Heather's table. "Hello," she said, with a smile. "You're Heather Prentiss, aren't you? We met earlier today, remember?"

Heather's blue-violet eyes regarded her over the rim of her coffee cup. How sad she looked, Liz thought.

After a moment's hesitation, Heather nodded. "Yes, I remember now. You were with the medical examiner this morning. Are you a policewoman?"

"No, I work in the medical examiner's office. My name is Liz Rooney. Do you mind if I join you?"

"I'd welcome the company," Heather said. She sighed. "I know you're wondering if my sister came home. She didn't. Not yet."

"I know this is a difficult time for you," Liz said, seating herself. "Do you have family to help you through this?"

Heather shook her head. "No. My sister and I— we've been on our own since we were nineteen. Our parents were killed in a car accident and we have no close relatives."

Liz studied the beautiful, sad face. This was a

start. "You must feel terribly alone now. Have you lived in Manhattan long?" she asked.

"No. We moved here from Florida just two weeks ago."

Only two weeks ago, Liz thought. This would seem to negate Heather's missing twin as an Ormsby cast-off, but she still had a feeling that Clover had been dumped by him. Something like that must have happened for Eichle and Rothman to connect her to the poisoning. Maybe Heather would tell her what she'd told them.

"What brought you to New York?" she asked.

"Clover insisted on moving up here," Heather replied. "She wanted to move to New York to be near a man she'd fallen in love with."

Liz's instincts quickened. This was the connection. But Heather and Clover had only been here for two weeks. She wanted to find out what else might have happened during that short time, but too many questions might make Heather clam up. A casual statement would be better.

"Somehow I get the feeling you would rather have stayed in Florida," she said.

Heather nodded. "Things were going great for us in Florida. Clover and I are both photographers' models. We had almost more work than we could handle."

"Being twins, I guess you were in great demand for television commercials."

"Yes, but we found it more satisfying to work as individuals. We made plenty of money. We bought a lovely condo near the beach. We had everything we wanted." She paused. A bitter expression crossed her face. "And then she met this New York guy."

It looked as if Heather had started to talk freely, Liz thought. Her anticipation heightened when, without any more questioning, Heather's words began to roll.

"She met him while she was doing a photo shoot at a yacht marina in Fort Lauderdale. She was on a break, coming back from the ladies' room in the clubhouse. She was walking along the dock when this good-looking guy got off his yacht just as she was passing by. They started talking, and that was the start of it. He was in Fort Lauderdale for over a week and he took her out every night and I guess he would have been around in the daytime too, but we were working. Anyway, he led her to believe he was in love with her. He asked her to move to New York. She was sure he wanted to marry her."

Heather's blue-violet eyes brimmed with tears. "She should have known he was only stringing her along when she didn't hear from him after he left Florida. Instead, she said he hadn't been gone very long and she'd hear from him any day now. Then when she still didn't hear from him she said he might be on another trip, and by the time he got back we'd be in New York, ourselves, and she'd surprise him by calling him and telling him we'd moved."

"What did you think of this man?" Liz asked.

"I never saw him," Heather replied. "Clover always met him somewhere and when she came home I was asleep. She wouldn't even tell me his name. She said I'd find out when we got to New York and she had a diamond engagement ring on her finger." She gave a bitter laugh. "What a lovesick little fool. As soon as we got to New York she tried to contact him but she couldn't ever get through to him and he never answered any of her calls."

Liz reflected on this. Judson had probably taken the calls and relayed the messages, and Ormsby had not bothered to respond. But on that ill-fated morning, Clover must have phoned after Judson left and Ormsby had picked up.

She recalled Judson saying Ormsby always remained on good terms with all his ex-ladyloves. He'd agreed to see Clover, planning to tell her they'd had a wonderful time together in Florida, but she'd misunderstood his intentions. He probably kept a few handsome parting gifts on hand for just such occasions. What had he chosen for Clover? A diamond bracelet?

"And your sister never told you this man's name— even after she realized he wasn't in love with her?"

Heather shook her head. "She refused to tell me. But I know now who he was. The detectives told me he's that rich man who was poisoned." Again, tears filled her eyes. "It's so horrible. They think Clover did it and they think she committed suicide."

"What do *you* think?" Liz asked.

Heather dabbed at her eyes with a tissue and gave a deep sigh. "I don't know. Clover was like a different person after we got to Manhattan and he wouldn't return her phone calls. She got terribly depressed, but in my heart I don't believe she poisoned him or killed herself, either. I think she might be out there, somewhere. Maybe she has amnesia."

Amnesia— This was a new twist, Liz thought. But it wasn't entirely out of the question. She wondered if Eichle and Rothman had thought of it. She thought of Clover's possible suicide again. If she had jumped off a rooftop or shot herself, her body would have been found by now. The same held true if she had checked into a hotel and taken an overdose of sleeping pills. But if she'd thrown herself into one of the rivers it could be a long time before her body was found—if it ever was.

Despite Heather's firm belief that Clover was alive somewhere, she must have thought of all these possibilities. It was hard to tell what thoughts lay behind those sad, violet eyes. *A young woman alone in a strange city, wondering if her missing twin sister was a murderer, wondering what had happened to her.* Suddenly she forgot she'd approached Heather to get information about the case. She only wanted to befriend her.

She reached across the table and touched Heather's hand. "I want to help you through this," she said. She tore a sheet of paper out of her notebook, wrote her home and work phone numbers on it, and handed it to Heather, saying, "If you ever feel you need to talk to someone, or if you just want company, please call me."

"Thank you." Heather took the paper and put it in her purse. Her eyes grew moist again. "You're very kind," she said. "It's been awful since Clover disappeared. I've been so lonely and frightened. I hate going back to our empty apartment."

"I have an idea," Liz said. "I'm on my way home now and I was going to fix myself some dinner. How about coming with me? It won't be anything fancy, but at least you wouldn't have to eat alone tonight."

Heather's eyes brightened. "If you're sure it wouldn't be too much trouble…"

Liz unlocked the door of her second floor walk-up and led Heather into the room which served as bedroom, living room, and eating area. She'd hidden the kitchenette with a three-panel screen. With her parents' old furniture, she'd managed to create a cozy, attractive place. "Make yourself at home while I get dinner started," she said. She went behind the screen and opened the refrigerator.

"What a nice apartment," Heather said. "Oh, and

you have a view of a pretty little park. Our apartment looks out on a busy street and a row of ugly buildings."

"Where's your place?" Liz asked.

"Forty-first Street near Lexington. It's a nice apartment, though. I'd like you to see it before I move back to Florida."

It was understandable she'd want to move back, Liz thought, as she fashioned chopped beef into hamburgers.

"But of course I won't leave till Clover's found," Heather said.

She spoke so calmly, Liz thought. It was as if this whole tragic situation hadn't fully sunk in. It was going to be terrible for her when she identified Clover in the morgue, if it ever happened, and perhaps even worse if Clover were found alive and brought back to face charges of murder. Either way, it would be rough on Heather.

"Are we going to eat at this gateleg table? Shall I open it up and set it while you're busy in the kitchen?" Heather asked.

Liz peered around the side of the screen. "Sure. Thanks. Silverware, place mats, and paper napkins are in the drawer of that cabinet next to the window."

When Heather finished setting the table, she joined Liz behind the screen. "Thank you for asking me to eat with you," she said. "I feel as if I've found a friend."

Liz's heart went out to her. "You have," she replied.

"I'm glad you're not a policewoman," Heather said. "I don't think we could be friends if you were. I'd feel like you were only being nice to me to get information about Clover."

A surge of guilt swept over Liz. It was gone in an instant. True, she'd started out only to get information about Clover, but strong feelings of empathy had taken over. Now she also wanted to do what she could to ease Heather's distress.

While they ate, Heather told her how close she and Clover were. "It's true what they say about identical twins," she said. "We express the same thoughts at the same time and buy each other the exact same Christmas and birthday presents. It's as if we're separate halves of a whole unit."

Liz had heard other twins describe the bond between them in a similar way. "I suppose you dressed alike too," she said.

Heather shook her head. "That's the only way we aren't like most identical twins. We both want to express our individuality."

She looked across the room at the shelves where Liz had displayed an array of photos. "Are those pictures of your family?" she asked.

"Yes. They're shots of my parents and my brother and me. Some were taken when we were kids."

"Are your parents still living?" Heather asked.

"Oh, sure. My father was a cop—a homicide detective. He retired from the force a couple of years ago and now he and my mother are having a ball cruising all over the country in their motor home. They're checking out places to settle down. Right now they're in Arizona."

"And your brother—where's he?"

"He lives in Los Angeles. He's an attorney."

"You're almost as alone as I am," Heather said. "Except you can talk to your parents and brother on the phone. I'll never talk to my parents again."

Liz noticed she didn't say, "Or Clover, either."

Heather shifted her gaze to a nearby table where Liz had placed a photo of Wade and herself. It had been taken at a party shortly after they met, before Wade got so critical of her interest in murder cases. "Is that your boyfriend?" Heather asked.

"He was until very recently," Liz replied. "I haven't gotten around to putting away that picture."

She didn't want to go into details, and was thankful when Heather changed the subject, saying, "I had a nice boyfriend in Florida. I should never have left him to come up here."

"Maybe when you go back to Florida you can pick up where you left off," Liz said. "He knows it was Clover who insisted you move, doesn't he?"

"He didn't believe me," Heather replied.

"Why don't you write to him and tell him you made a mistake going with Clover and you'll be back?" Liz asked.

"I don't know if I should. He was very angry. He might tear the letter up or send it back unopened," Heather replied.

"You could phone him," Liz suggested. "And tell him, quickly, before he had a chance to hang up on you."

"Maybe I'll try that," Heather said. She rose from her chair. "I must be going. If another woman's body is brought into the morgue, Detective Eichle might be trying to reach me. He's convinced that Clover is dead."

But Heather was just as sure Clover was alive, Liz thought.

At the door, Heather said, "Thanks so much, Liz. You really cheered me up. I'll phone you soon about having dinner at *my* place."

From the window, Liz watched her hail a cab in front of the building. Forming a friendship with Heather was the last thing she'd expected, but now that it seemed to be developing, she felt pleased. Heather needed a friend. As for herself, with Sophie seeing more and more of Ralph, and Wade out of her life, she'd have plenty of time on her hands. Besides, Heather was good company.

FIVE

Sophie called her at the office the next morning. "Rothman and Eichle are getting a lot of heat from the D.A. for not making an arrest in the Ormsby case," she said. "The D.A.'s with them now, talking about it."

"How can he expect an arrest when the prime suspect is missing and presumed dead?" Liz asked.

"Don't ask me—all I know is what I overhear," Sophie replied. "How did it go with Heather? Did you find out anything else about her missing twin?"

"Not really. She seemed so pathetic, I didn't want to push it. But I took her back to my place for dinner and we plan to get together again soon, so maybe she'll volunteer something without my asking a lot of questions."

"Sounds like you made friends with her."

"I did. She doesn't know a soul up here and she needs someone to talk to till she goes back to Florida."

"Is she going back? I don't think Rothman and Eichle know about that."

"She said she plans to go back after her sister's

found. She thinks Clover's alive somewhere and might have amnesia."

"Yeah, right," Sophie said. "Well, I gotta go. Can you meet me after work? Ralph's on duty tonight, so maybe we could grab something to eat early and catch a movie afterwards; unless you've made up with Wade and you're seeing him tonight."

"Wade's permanently out of the picture, so we're on."

"Okay. See you later at the newsstand. Meanwhile, I'll try and pick up some more about the D.A. pressing for an arrest."

Liz ARRIVED at the newsstand first. She bought the *Daily News* and scanned the front page. Bye Bye Mr. Big Bucks, the headline screamed. Ormsby's funeral had taken place that morning. A few lines of text described the service as private, attended by a few close friends and associates.

As she glanced at the photo of his casket being borne out of the Ormsby family's church, Sophie arrived. "Oh, you're reading about the funeral," she said. "Eichle went."

Liz looked at the newspaper again. "It says here the service was private—but I suppose Eichle would go, anyway. I guess he wanted to see who was there. Remember that murder I followed last year where the killer was nabbed at the funeral?"

Sophie nodded. "Eichle should be so lucky." She

paused, frowning slightly. "I have something to tell you."

"Sounds as if I'm not going to like it," Liz said, as they started walking to the restaurant.

"No, you won't like it," Sophie said. "Remember I told you the D.A.'s pressing for an arrest? Well, he's coming down on Judson."

"Oh, no! Did you hear why?"

"Judson's taking medicine with the same stuff in it that was found in Ormsby's system during the autopsy. It sounds like they're going to go ahead and build a case against him."

"Surely the D.A. doesn't believe that poor old man did it."

"It's politics," Sophie said. "He's coming up for reelection and he wants an arrest. He knows he won't get one by assuming a missing person is the guilty party."

Liz shook her head. "This will be devastating to Judson."

"Rothman said if Judson's arrested he'll get out on bail and Eichle said the charges might be dropped after the election. All the D.A. wants is a quick arrest to brag about during the campaign."

"That won't undo the damage to that poor old man," Liz said. "To be accused of poisoning someone he's served so faithfully all these years…"

"I know, it's a shame, but I heard Rothman quote the D.A. as saying the evidence against the missing twin is circumstantial, and even if they find her body, it would be a flimsy case."

"It's not more circumstantial or flimsy than the evidence against Judson. They both had motive and opportunity, but Judson has been devoted to Ormsby for years."

"The difference is he's here and Clover isn't," Sophie said.

Surely Rothman and Eichle hadn't ruled out the possibility that Clover was on the run, Liz thought. But even if she were found alive, poor old Judson would already have been put through humiliation and heartbreak.

In the restaurant, they chose a quiet booth where they could discuss this further. "Suppose Clover didn't commit suicide," Liz said. "Where would she have gone?"

"Not Florida, that's for sure. Maybe someplace else where they used to live."

Heather and Clover had plenty of money, Liz thought. Clover could have gone anywhere she pleased. She could be in some foreign country by now.

"Eichle and Rothman must have gotten the previous addresses from Heather," Liz said. "They must have started investigating. Even though it's unlikely Clover would have gone to any of those places, at least they should have some information about her by this time." School records would provide insight into Clover's personality, she thought.

Sophie shook her head. "According to what I overheard, they started investigating, but the Prentiss family had lived in three different cities. Before they could come up with anything, the D.A. ordered the investigation dropped."

"And told them to go after Judson."

"Maybe something will break before he's indicted," Sophie said.

Liz sighed. "I hope you're right." But with the medicine as evidence, she knew a case against Judson could be put together quickly.

After eating, they hopped a cab to a theatre that showed old movies. Tonight, one of their favorites was playing—*Casablanca*. They'd seen it several times, but it had been more than a year since their last viewing. "It's time for a *Casablanca* fix," Sophie had said, when they discussed which movie they wanted to see tonight.

Afterwards, they went for a snack at a fast-food place. By the time Liz got back to her apartment, it was almost ten o'clock. She checked for messages on her machine and found she had three with Wade's caller ID number displayed. For a moment she considered ignoring it, but decided she'd see what he had to say.

The first two messages asked her to call him back. In the third his voice sounded annoyed. "Where have you been, Liz? I've been trying to get you all evening. Give me a call when you get in, if it's not too late."

"It *is* too late, Wade, for us," she muttered. But she thought it only common courtesy to return his calls. He answered on the first ring.

"Hi, Wade," she said.

"Where in blazes have you been?" he asked.

"I don't like the tone of your voice or the question either," she replied.

"Sorry. Now will you tell me where you were?"

"I had dinner with Sophie and we went to a movie."

"I suppose Sophie the super female cop clued you in on your latest murder, as usual," he said, with a trace of a snarl.

Liz suddenly felt belligerent. "Why did you phone me, Wade? Didn't you badger me enough the other night?"

"It's not about that," he replied. "I hoped we could get together and talk things over."

"What's there to talk over, Wade?"

"I can't believe you want to give up on a meaningful relationship because of your obsession with homicide cases. We need to discuss this. I'm coming over right now."

"There's nothing to discuss," she said, "and it's been quite a while since I found anything meaningful in our relationship. It's late. I'm going to bed." She glanced at her watch. The ten-o'clock news would be on TV in a minute. She wanted to find out if there were any new developments in the Ormsby case. "I'm hanging up now, Wade," she said, and did.

In her mind's eye she could see his handsome face clouded with anger. She knew she'd never hear from him again. She turned on the TV. The news broadcast had just started. Her heart sank when she heard the first item.

"Charles Judson, longtime servant of billionaire playboy Theodore Van Brunt Ormsby, was arrested tonight in connection with Ormsby's murder."

SIX

LIZ'S PHONE WAS RINGING when she got to her desk the next morning. Intuition told her it would be Heather. She must have heard about Judson's arrest.

Her instincts were right on the mark.

"Does this mean they don't think Clover did it?" Heather asked.

"I guess so," Liz replied. A sudden thought struck her. Maybe Eichle and Rothman's quick action was strategy. Maybe they believed Clover was really the guilty one and if she were, indeed, alive somewhere, she'd come out of hiding when she heard someone else had been arrested.

Heather's voice broke into her thoughts. "I feel terribly lonesome, Liz. I need company. Can we have dinner tonight at my place?"

"Sure. What time?"

"Come after work." She gave her address.

"Okay," Liz said. "See you later."

She'd barely hung up when Sophie called. "I know you heard Judson's been arrested."

"Yes. Poor old man."

"You don't think there's a chance he did it?"

"I think it's much more likely Clover did."

"Anything new in that department? Have you heard from Heather?"

"I'm having dinner at her place tonight."

"Sounds like you two are getting chummy—or are you just getting information?"

"A little of both. But whatever information I get, it won't be because I pushed for it. I'll fill you in next time we get together."

"Okay—how about tomorrow after work? We can talk over coffee before I meet Ralph. Are you still on the outs with Wade?"

"Yes—it's permanent." She described last night's phone conversation.

"So, it's really over with you two," Sophie said. "Too bad. He was kind of stuffy, but otherwise he seemed like a nice guy."

"He is a nice guy," Liz replied. "Probably too nice for the likes of someone whose passion is trying to solve murder cases. I wish him well. I hope he finds a woman whose hobby is crocheting pot holders."

Sophie laughed. "Well, look at it this way. If you hadn't broken up with him at this particular time, you might not be having dinner at Heather's place tonight. I can't wait till tomorrow to hear if you found out anything else about Clover. Call me the minute you get home tonight. I gotta go now."

What would she do without Sophie's input? Liz wondered, as she hung up the phone. She'd helped make this case the most interesting ever. She hoped Eichle never found out that she and Sophie were best friends. He'd be sure and put two and two together.

DURING THE MORNING Dan came into her office. "I ran into Wade on the elevator this morning," he said.

"Did he tell you we broke up?"

Dan nodded. "Yes. I'm sorry it didn't work out. Edna was sure the two of you would hit it off."

"Well, we could have if he hadn't started giving me a bad time about my interest in murder cases. He said it was morbid and unfeminine and his mother would never approve."

Dan cast her a grin. "It would take a lot more than that to make you unfeminine, Lizzie."

She laughed. "Thanks for the kind words. Maybe someday I'll meet a man who agrees with you."

"Meanwhile, don't let anyone make you give up what interests you," Dan said, on his way out the door. "Especially someone with a disapproving mother."

AFTER WORK, on the way to the subway, she passed a newsstand. A headline from the *Daily News* shouted at her. The Butler Did It??? She didn't buy a copy. Just thinking about poor old Judson's arrest was bad enough; she didn't need to read about it.

It was only a short walk from the subway station to Heather's apartment building, an old but well-maintained structure. It was equipped with a buzzer entry system. Heather answered right away. "Come on up, Liz," she said. "Take the elevator. Apartment 2-A is to the right."

She opened her door with a sad smile. "I'm glad you're here," she said. "I've been feeling blue all day. I miss Clover so much." Following Heather through a small foyer into a spacious living room, Liz noticed boxes and cartons stacked all over the place. "Excuse the mess," Heather said. "We hadn't finished unpacking when Clover disappeared and since then I just haven't felt like it. Anyway, I'll be moving back to Florida. No use unpacking and repacking all over again."

"You have a nice apartment," Liz said, seating herself on a tan tapestry sofa and glancing around the room. The sofa, the two green-and-tan plaid armchairs, the beige carpet and dark wood tables didn't suggest Florida, she thought. This must be a furnished apartment.

Heather's next comment bore this out. "We were lucky to find this partially furnished apartment on the Internet," she said, sitting down on the sofa. "We didn't have to move much of our own stuff up here and we rented our Florida condo furnished, so the move back won't be too much of a hassle."

On a table next to the sofa, a photo of a man and a woman and two little girls caught Liz's eyes. "Is that you and Clover with your parents?" she asked.

"Yes. It was taken when we were about six."

Heather and Clover were indeed identical, Liz thought, looking at the two little faces so uncannily alike. She noticed they wore matching outfits and hair ribbons.

"Our mother enjoyed dressing us alike when we were little," Heather said. "But when we were teenagers we rebelled and refused to go along with that anymore."

"Do you have photos of you and Clover during your rebellious teens?" Liz asked.

Heather glanced towards the cartons. "Most of our pictures are still packed away. I'll try and find them to show you when you come next time." She smiled. "I hope we can get together a few more times before I go back to Florida."

Liz nodded. "We will." Again she thought Heather was talking a lot about moving.

"I'm making a pasta dish for dinner," Heather said. "I hope you like pasta."

"Sure," Liz replied. "Anything with pasta is okay with me."

Heather rose from the sofa. "Come on out in the kitchen with me while I put on the finishing touches."

Liz followed her into a large kitchen with up-to-date appliances and plenty of cabinets and counter space. More evidence of Heather and Clover's secure financial status. The rent on this place had to be three times what she was paying for her place.

Heather looked into the oven. "It's not quite ready," she said. "How about something to drink while we're waiting? Soda, beer, wine…?"

"Beer would be fine, thanks."

"I like beer too," Heather said, taking two bottles out of the fridge. "So does Clover. This is her favorite brand."

Liz noted she'd said, "So does Clover." She'd been referring to her twin sister in the present tense all along. Of course it was possible Clover actually did have amnesia as the result of an accident, but had it occurred to her that Clover might be a fugitive?

While they ate, they talked about their jobs. Heather's career as a photographer's model sounded glamorous, Liz thought. "Did you and Clover look into getting modeling jobs in Manhattan?" she asked.

Heather shook her head. "I planned to do that after we got settled, but all Clover did after we got here was try and get in touch with that man." Abruptly, she changed the subject. "For dessert I got an apple pie at the bakery down the block. Do you like coffee with dessert?"

"I can take it or leave it, so please don't go to the trouble of making it unless you want it, yourself."

"I haven't been drinking coffee at night, lately,"

Heather replied. "I've been having trouble getting to sleep and coffee just makes it worse."

It was understandable that worry about Clover would keep Heather wakeful, Liz thought.

When they finished dinner they went into the living room and continued their conversation. Listening to Liz talk about Mom and Pop, Heather gave a wistful smile. "You're so lucky to have both your parents living, even though they're not nearby."

"I can only imagine what a terrible shock it was for you and Clover when your parents were killed," Liz said.

"We were devastated," Heather replied. "We were such a close family. Clover and I were just starting to get over it when she met that man." She shook her head as if to rid her mind of the painful thought.

At that moment, the downstairs buzzer sounded. Heather went to answer it, saying, "I don't know who that could be. I don't know anyone in New York except you and Detective Eichle."

A few moments later Liz heard a man's voice. "I hope you don't mind my dropping in like this, Miss Prentiss." The voice was George Eichle's.

When Heather let him into the apartment, Liz heard her say, "I understand the servant was arrested. I didn't think you'd be questioning me anymore, Detective. I thought you'd decided Clover didn't do it."

They came into the living room. Eichle saw Liz.

Surprise and anger spread all over his face. "What are you doing here, Rooney?"

"What does it look like, Eichle?" she snapped back. "I'm visiting Heather."

Heather looked puzzled at the testy exchange. "Liz and I ran into each other at a coffee shop," she said. "We've become friends."

Liz rose from the sofa. "I guess I'd better leave, Heather, so the detective can get on with his questioning."

"Don't leave, Liz," Heather pleaded. "You can go into the bedroom while Detective Eichle is questioning me. There's a TV in there you can watch till he's finished."

"No need for that," Eichle said. "I'm not here to question you, Miss Prentiss. I just wanted to assure you we haven't stopped the search for your sister. It's true we've made an arrest, but that doesn't alter the fact that she's still missing and we're making every effort to find her."

"Thank you for not giving up the search," Heather said. "And thank you for coming to tell me. I'll always be grateful for the kind way you and Detective Rothman treated me, even when you thought Clover had killed Mr. Ormsby."

Liz glanced at Eichle to get his reaction to this expression of gratitude. She was surprised to catch a fleeting look in his eyes. It was gone in an instant, but she had no doubt of its meaning. *As far as Eichle was concerned, Clover was not yet off the hook!*

She stared at him, her mind teeming with questions. Had he arrested Judson only to go along with the D.A.? Had he decided to continue investigating Clover on his own?

Heather's voice broke into her thoughts. "Would you like a cup of coffee or something, Detective?"

"Thanks. Coffee would go great," he replied.

Liz glanced at her watch. Eichle was putting in some overtime on Clover. This not only reinforced her conviction that he still thought she was guilty, it firmed up her idea that he might be doing this on his own.

When Heather went to the kitchen to make the coffee, Liz stole a glance at him. He was looking around the room. Of course he noticed the boxes and cartons. "Heather told me Clover disappeared before they'd finished unpacking, and she hasn't felt up to finishing it yet," she said.

"I'll bet that's not all she told you after you bombarded her with questions," he replied.

Liz bristled. "I didn't bombard her with questions. Anything she told me came out in conversation."

"Are you trying to make me believe you didn't deliberately strike up a friendship to get information about the case?"

She knew there was no point in attempting to explain. He wouldn't believe what had started out as a fishing expedition was now a genuine wish to befriend Heather.

"Believe what you want to, Eichle," she said. "You're incapable of thinking beyond my interest in murder cases."

"What is it with you?" he asked. "Why can't you just let the police do the job and stop trying to play like that woman on television. At least she's supposed to be a mystery writer."

"And all I am is a clerk in the medical examiner's office?"

"I'm not denigrating your job, Rooney. I'm only saying you should keep your nose out of police business."

"Tell me exactly how following a case is interfering with police business."

"You show up everywhere. Take this particular case. You have no business at a crime scene or in the morgue when a suspect is shown for identification, and you certainly are out of line when you worm your way into the confidence of a suspect's sister."

His use of the word "worm" got her dander up. "For your information, Detective Eichle, when I accepted Heather's dinner invitation, I was under the impression that her sister was no longer a suspect." Not that she wouldn't have accepted it anyway, she thought, but he didn't have to know that.

"She's still a factor in the case," he said.

Police double-talk, she thought. "Are you telling me she's not a suspect anymore?" she asked.

"That's none of your business, either."

Her instincts were right, Liz decided. He hadn't written Clover off yet and he was continuing this investigation on his own. She couldn't resist taking a jab at him. "If I *worm* anything out of Heather tonight I'll be sure and let you know."

He seemed about to make a retort, but just then the kitchen door swung open and Heather came in with the coffee.

Eichle didn't linger over it. He drained his mug in a few minutes and said he had to leave. As he rose from his chair he glanced at Liz. "You need a lift home?"

He wanted to lambaste her some more about meddling in the case, she thought. "Thanks, but I'm not ready to leave yet," she replied.

"Better take a cab home," he said. "It's a dark walk to the subway and you shouldn't take a chance on being mugged or worse."

She could almost hear his counter jab in the words he left unspoken. *"You wouldn't be able to poke your nose into your own murder."*

"It's so kind of you to be concerned," she replied. "I'll take your advice."

With tonight's encounter his hostility towards her had swollen like air in an inflatable balloon. It would reach the bursting point if he ever found out about her friendship with Officer Sophie Pulaski.

SEVEN

LIZ GOT BACK TO HER apartment about nine. She hadn't found out much more about Clover, but she'd gained an insight into Heather. Bitterness towards "that man" lay beneath her calm surface. It was clear she blamed Ormsby for Clover's disappearance.

Eichle's unexpected arrival at Heather's apartment, and their heated exchange of words still rankled. Not that she expected him to encourage her interest in murder cases like Pop and Dan did, but he didn't have to make such an issue of it.

She watched TV for a while, hoping to catch some late-breaking news about the case. The only mention of it was a rehash of Judson's arrest. She should have told Eichle what she thought about that. It might have been the one topic they could discuss amicably. He wouldn't still be following up on Clover if he believed Judson had done the poisoning.

In the morning she remembered Sophie had asked her to phone when she got back from Heather's, and she hadn't. But most likely Sophie wouldn't have been home from her date with Ralph, anyway. She smiled, thinking of the countless crushes on boys she and Sophie had seen each other through. But it was different with Ralph. From the first, she sensed that Sophie would develop lasting feelings for him. It wouldn't surprise her if sometime soon Sophie told her they were getting married.

It would be the end of an era, she thought with a twinge of regret. Sure, she and Sophie would always be close and they'd see one another often, but once Sophie was caught up in wifehood, things would not be the same. With a wry smile, Liz told herself if she wanted to get on anywhere near their old footing, she'd have to get married too.

"Sorry I forgot to phone you when I got home last night," she said, when Sophie called her at the office. "But it was early. I'll bet you were still out."

"I was. I didn't get home till almost midnight," Sophie replied. "How did it go with Heather?"

Liz described the evening, including Eichle's unexpected appearance. "He told Heather he'd just dropped in to assure her they hadn't called off the search for Clover."

Sophie gave a snort of laughter. "Oh, right. He could have told her that over the phone. What do you suppose he was up to?"

"I think he hasn't ruled out Clover."

"You mean he might have decided to investigate her on his own?"

"Why else would he show up at Heather's apartment and be so ticked off when he found *me* there?" Liz replied. A thought flashed into her mind. She laughed. "Unless he's developed a thing for Heather."

Sophie laughed too. "That wouldn't be hard to do. Maybe you're on to something there, Liz."

"Maybe, but I think it's more likely he's just continuing to investigate Clover on his own."

"Well, if he is, he's putting it on hold for a few days. This morning I heard him tell Rothman he's taking some vacation time soon."

With Judson under arrest, as far as the D.A. was concerned the initial investigation was over, Liz thought. Eichle was free to take some time off.

"I heard something else this morning," Sophie said. "Judson's hearing is scheduled for this afternoon. He'll probably be released on bail."

"So soon?"

"Talk in Homicide is that Judson's arrest didn't sit well with the judge assigned to the hearing."

"Good for that judge! Even though they're supposed to be impartial, he did the right thing."

"According to what I heard, he said he stepped up the hearing because of Judson's age and health problems. If the hearing weren't held today, Judson would have to spend the weekend in jail. Oh, I also heard Rothman say the bail will probably be low."

"Good. Poor old man. I'm glad that judge has sense enough to realize he's not a menace to society." Nor was he likely to flee the country, she thought.

"So what are you doing over the weekend, Liz?"

"Nothing very exciting. How about you?"

"Ralph and I are both off tomorrow, and he's taking me to meet his family in Yonkers. We're leaving right after work today. We'll have dinner with them and stay overnight."

"Taking you home to Mother? Sounds serious."

"I'll decide how serious it is after I meet his family, especially his mother," Sophie said. "Suppose she turns out to be one of those dragon ladies you hear about? Well, I gotta go now. Sorry we can't meet for coffee today, but I'll call you later if I hear anything else about the case."

Her own weekend was going to be quiet bordering on dull, Liz thought, as she hung up the phone. For a moment, even a date with Wade looked good. But the moment passed. She'd catch up on her reading, take in an exhibit at one of the art museums, go over to Staten Island and visit her grandmother. She'd planned to call Heather, anyway, to thank her for the dinner. When she did, maybe Heather would suggest going to a movie or something. But she'd leave that up to Heather. She must be careful not to push.

After work she went directly to her apartment. She found a letter from Mom and Pop in her mailbox and didn't even wait till she got upstairs to open it. The letter, written in Mom's precise schoolteacher penmanship, said they were on the road again, heading east from Arizona. They'd decided the southwest desert was not for them. They were homesick for the seacoast.

"We checked out the area around Corpus Christi, Texas, yesterday and are on our way to look around the gulf coast of Florida," Mom wrote. "We'll call you soon." The letter was postmarked New Orleans, three days ago. Unless they'd stopped over for a while in New Orleans, they must be in Florida by now, Liz thought.

While she ate a microwaved frozen dinner, she read the letter through, again. If Mom and Pop were still living in the big old house on Staten Island, she could hop the ferry tomorrow and be with them over the weekend. She could sleep in her room with the pink flowered wallpaper and the white organdy curtains. She could help Mom get meals ready in the homey old kitchen. She could watch a ball game with Pop.

A visit to Grandma McGowan might ease some of her sudden nostalgia, she thought. Though she and Grandma talked on the phone regularly, Liz realized with a rush of regret that she hadn't been to visit her since Christmas. She'd give her a call tonight and ask if it would be convenient for her to drop by tomorrow or Sunday.

The phone call was disappointing. Grandma would be away over the weekend. She was leaving tomorrow on a bus trip to Atlantic City with her garden club. Look on the bright side, Liz told herself. With no distractions for the next two days she'd have plenty of time to think about the case of the poisoned playboy. She might even make her own definite decision as to who did it.

She mulled her own suspects over in her mind. Clover topped the list, of course, but she hadn't ruled out Dr. Hammond and Cherie La Salle. Though there was evidence against Judson, it was flimsy. If a judge thought he should never have been arrested, that was good enough for her. She decided to cross him off the list.

The jangle of the phone broke into her thoughts. She almost wept with joy when she heard Mom's voice, and then Pop's. They were in Sarasota, Florida.

"Ask Dan if you can take some vacation time on short notice," Pop said. "We want you to fly down and visit us for a few days."

She'd never moved so fast in her life. First, a phone call to Dan. Next, her reservation on a flight leaving Sunday morning. Then, a quick wardrobe survey and a frantic hunt for the key to her luggage. Tomorrow she'd phone Sophie's house and leave a message with Mrs. Pulaski about her sudden departure. She'd also phone Heather. She hoped Heather wouldn't feel homesick knowing she was going to Florida.

WHEN SHE CALLED HEATHER the next day she sensed the sadness in her voice. "Thanks for letting me know," Heather said. "I would have phoned you and wondered where you were." She sighed. "Florida. I wish I were going too. I wish I didn't have to stay here and wait for word from Detective Eichle. I want to get back to my boyfriend."

Evidently she didn't know yet that Eichle was going on vacation, Liz thought. But if anything turned up regarding Clover, Rothman would tell her.

She could hardly wait till she could discuss the case with Pop. Just thinking about it made her happy.

EIGHT

POP DROVE THE TAURUS through the entrance of the RV park, saying, "I guess you've been following that case where the billionaire was poisoned, haven't you, Lizzie?"

She'd wanted to discuss the case during the drive from the airport, but he and Mom never stopped talking about all the places they'd seen and the places they planned to see. "I guess you heard all about it and you knew I'd have to get into that one," she replied.

"The story was in the Arizona newspapers and of course it was on TV," Mom said. "I must say it seemed like a baffling case with that mysterious woman the guard saw go up to the penthouse and then her sister showing up at police headquarters saying she was missing and might have committed suicide. When I read that I said to myself the missing sister did it. But now they know who did it, don't they? They arrested the houseman."

"Yes, he was arrested, but I don't believe he did it."

"Who do you think did it?" Pop asked. "The missing sister?"

Liz nodded. Evidently the police still hadn't released the names of the sisters, and they were still withholding the fact that the sisters were identical twins. Should she tell Pop what she knew? Discussing the case with him wouldn't be as much fun if she didn't. But she didn't want to reveal confidential information.

"The missing sister's my prime suspect. I met Judson the houseman face-to-face and I can tell you he was devastated. Poor old man—he was devoted to Ormsby. I just can't imagine him doing such a thing."

Pop chuckled. "How many times have I told you a good detective never lets himself or herself feel sorry for a suspect?"

Liz smiled. "And how many times have I told you I have no intentions of becoming a detective? I'm into this purely for fun."

"A lot of good sleuthing talent going to waste," Pop replied. He slowed the car. "There's our trailer just ahead, the one on the right, under the big tree."

"Frank, when are you going to stop calling it a trailer?" Mom scolded. "The really nice ones are called mobile homes." And theirs was a nice one. Liz had seen it before they set forth on their travels. It had all the comforts of a small house—two bedrooms, two baths, an efficient kitchen, and a big-screen TV in the living area.

Pop stopped the Taurus next to it. "Welcome to

our *mobile home,* Lizzie," he said, casting a grin at Mom.

By the time Liz unpacked it was noon. Mom made salad and grilled cheese sandwiches for lunch. They ate outside at a table in the shade of the live oak.

"Were you lucky enough to find parks as nice as this everywhere you went?" Liz asked.

"Most of the time," Mom replied. "I'd recommend mobile-home life to anyone. We've been having a ball."

"We were wise to decide on a trailer," Pop said. "If we'd bought one of those big bus homes, we wouldn't be able to explore the areas as easily. This way we can just unhook and take off."

Liz knew he was teasing Mom, saying "trailer" again, and referring to motor homes as bus homes. "Have you done much exploring around here yet?" she asked.

"We spent all day yesterday looking around," Mom replied. "Sarasota is a beautiful city. I feel like we could have a good life here."

"Do you think you might buy a house here?"

"Possibly," Pop said. "But we want to check out other places in Florida. I thought we'd take a run over to the east coast tomorrow and see what Fort Lauderdale looks like. We'll stay overnight in a motel. That'll give us plenty of time to check out all the places."

Fort Lauderdale! Liz's senses went on alert.

"What's that look on your face?" Pop asked.

"The missing sister and the other one are from Fort Lauderdale," she replied.

Pop cast her a knowing grin. "I see. And what else did you find out?"

She couldn't hold back any longer. She had to tell him everything. Telling him would be telling Mom too, but as the wife of a former police detective she'd be as closemouthed about it as he. "The sisters are identical twins. The one who reported her sister missing is named Heather. The missing twin's name is Clover."

"Twins!" Mom exclaimed. "That makes the case even more interesting."

Pop's grin broadened. "Last I heard, the police weren't divulging the names of the sisters, and nothing was said about them being twins. How come you know so much?"

"I made friends with Heather," Liz replied. She told about going to the morgue with Dan, her chance encounter with Heather in the coffee shop, and everything else.

"Nice going, Lizzie," he said. "But that doesn't explain the look on your face. What are you up to?"

"Heather and Clover moved to New York only a couple of weeks ago."

"I get it. You want to do a little investigating while we're here."

"Right. Their address would still be in the phone

book. Maybe I could go to their old neighborhood and very discreetly ask some questions about Clover."

Pop looked dubious. "You could try, but I wouldn't count on getting much information that way."

"I thought someone might have noticed something strange about Clover. Heather said she was in a depressed state because Ormsby broke her heart. I want to find out if she was already in a depression before she left Florida. If she was, it must have gotten worse after she got to New York and Ormsby wouldn't return her calls. It could have driven her to kill him and then kill herself."

"Who's on the case?" Pop asked.

"Eichle and Rothman."

"They're both smart enough to have picked up on that. I'm surprised they arrested the houseman before getting more background on the missing twin."

"They were pressured into it. The D.A. needed an arrest to help him get reelected. I think Eichle agrees with me that Clover's a likely suspect. I'm pretty sure he's continuing to investigate her on his own."

"Didn't you tell me Eichle was giving you a bad time about you showing up at homicide scenes? Are you two getting along better now?"

"No. If anything, he's more hostile than ever. I just happen to think we see eye to eye about Clover."

She wanted to talk some more with Pop about going to the twins' neighborhood, but Mom broke into the conversation. "With all this talk about your murder case, you haven't told us how you're doing, Liz. Do you still like your job?"

"I love my job," Liz replied. "Dan's the greatest boss ever. He let me go with him to the Ormsby murder scene and…" She stopped short with a smile. "Sorry, Mom. I know you've heard enough about the case for a while."

"Yes, I have," Mom said. "I'm glad you like your job. How about your apartment? Are you still comfortable in that tiny space?"

"Sure, Mom. It's all I need."

"How's Sophie?"

"Great. We meet for coffee almost every day after work. She's been seeing a really nice man—a cop— and I think it's getting serious."

"Are you still seeing that man Dan and Edna introduced you to?"

"No. We broke up a couple of days ago. But it's okay, Mom. I was the one who wanted to end it."

"I thought you liked him."

"I did at first, but it didn't work out. He didn't understand my interest in solving murder cases and he kept hassling me about it till I just couldn't take any more of it."

Mom was silent for a moment. "If a homicide detective doesn't go along with your gruesome hobby, how could you expect a civilian to understand it?" she asked.

"Now don't *you* start giving her a bad time too, Marge," Pop said.

Mom gave an apologetic smile. "Sorry, dear."

Liz knew what she was thinking. Two men had already made clear their objections to her "gruesome hobby." Mom thought it would keep her from forming a lasting relationship.

Pop must have read Mom's thoughts too. He changed the subject. "After lunch, what do you say we take a drive and show Liz that new development we liked yesterday?"

"Fine," Mom replied. "I think you'll like it too, Liz. It's a gated community with a golf course, tennis courts, pool, and clubhouse."

"We're planning on having you visit us often," Pop said.

"Sounds like you've almost made up your mind."

Mom nodded. "But we heard such glowing reports about Fort Lauderdale, we want to check it out before we decide."

THEY GOT TO Fort Lauderdale shortly before noon the next day.

"A couple we met in Arizona told us about a lovely restaurant right on the waterfront," Mom said. "I think we should have lunch there." She fumbled in her purse. "I wrote the name down. It's in here some-where…." She looked at Pop. "Do you remember the name, Frank?"

"No, but I remember they said it was right near a big marina. I need to fill up the tank anyway. I'll ask at the gas station."

A big marina. Liz's imagination raced. It might be the same one where billionaire playboy Theodore Van Brunt Ormsby disembarked from his yacht and encountered beautiful photographer's model Clover Prentiss. Maybe another photographic shoot would be taking place there today. Maybe the camera crew would be the same one that worked with Clover that day. Maybe she could question them. They might have noticed if Clover was subject to mood swings. Maybe one of them would say she seemed depressed.

She realized the chances of any of this were remote. There were too many maybes, she told herself. But that was what made following murder cases so interesting.

While these thoughts crowded her mind, Pop pulled into a gas station. The manager said the marina with the good restaurant nearby had to be Bahia Mar. He gave directions.

When Liz saw the rows of trim yachts tied up in their slips she felt sure this was the same marina where Clover was doing the TV commercial the day she met Ormsby. She scanned the docks for some sign of video and audio equipment. Nothing. But of course TV commercials weren't shot here all the time, she told herself. Most likely there hadn't been any at this marina since the one Clover made before she and Heather left Fort Lauderdale.

In the restaurant, Pop gave her a searching look. "You've hardly said a word since we sat down, Liz. You've got that case on your mind, haven't you?"

"I can't stop thinking about it, Pop—especially now that I'm right here where it all began."

"When we check into the motel you can look up the twins' address in the phone book. If you really want to question their neighbors, we'll go there to-morrow morning."

"Oh, Pop. Thank you!"

Mom gave a sigh. "We're here to look at real estate, Frank."

"We have plenty of time to look around this after-noon," he replied. "And after Liz does her investigat-ing tomorrow, we'll look some more before we head back to Sarasota."

AFTER AN AFTERNOON spent looking at houses and condos, they checked into adjoining rooms in a motel. The first thing Liz did was grab a telephone book. There was no listing for Prentiss. "They probably had an unlisted number," Pop said. "But being models, they must have worked through an agency. You'd get more information about Clover from the agency than from neighbors."

"Good idea, Pop. I'll look it up," Liz said. She

found a listing for a modeling agency in the vicinity.

"We'll drive there in the morning," Pop said. "It shouldn't take you long to ask your questions, and then we'll be on our way to look at real estate."

"Thanks for indulging me, Pop."

"To tell the truth, I'm getting caught up in this case, myself," he replied, with a laugh. "But, a word of advice: Don't go into the agency with a barrage of questions right off the bat. You won't get anywhere. Make it seem as if you're trying to locate two old friends. Most folks want to be helpful. Chances are you'll get plenty of information that way, and then if you need to you can follow up with a few well-chosen questions."

THE MODELING AGENCY was located in a multistory building in a business area. Pop pulled the Taurus into a nearby parking lot. Mom had already spied a gift shop down the block and said she'd do some browsing while Liz was occupied.

"I'll wait for you in the car," Pop said. "I want to look at a map, anyway."

Liz entered the building and paused beneath the directory. The modeling agency was on the fourth floor, suite four-twelve. As she turned and made her way to the elevator, she heard a familiar voice.

"Rooney! What are you doing in Fort Lauderdale?"

It couldn't be anyone but George Eichle. She turned around. He looked more surprised than angry. "I might ask you the same question, Eichle," she replied.

They glared at each other. She knew why he was in Fort Lauderdale. He was conducting his own investigation of Clover while pretending to be on vacation. And she knew he suspected she'd come here for the same reason.

Eichle broke the silence. "I happen to be here on vacation."

"And I happen to be visiting my parents in Sarasota. We drove over here yesterday to look at real estate."

His face softened. "Your folks are here?"

"Yes, Pop's waiting for me in the car."

He didn't ask what she was doing in the building. He'd already guessed, she thought. "I was just on my way out," he said. "Where's your car? I'd like to say hello to your father." There was no point in her going up to the modeling agency now, she decided. The story about trying to locate her two friends wouldn't fly after Eichle had been up there, flashing his police badge and asking questions about the same two. The early bird had gotten the worm.

"I know Pop would like to see you too," she said. "Come on out to the parking lot with me."

"Weren't you about to get on the elevator?" he asked, with a wry smile.

She'd never seen any kind of a smile on his face before. Even a wry one was better than the dour looks she always got. He knew she'd been on her way up to the modeling agency, but he wasn't making a big deal of it.

"I've changed my mind," she said.

The wry smile deepened, telling her he knew why.

She pretended not to notice. "Let's go out to the car so you can say hello to Pop."

Pop was studying a map of Florida when they approached the Taurus. His face broke into a broad smile when he saw Eichle. After the jovial greetings, the handshakes and the backslapping, Liz told them she'd go and join Mom in the gift shop. "You guys have a lot of catching up to do," she said. As she left, she cast a warning glance at Pop. His answering glance told her he understood. If Eichle said anything about the Ormsby case, he'd clam up.

On her way to the gift shop she passed the building where the modeling agency was located. She noticed a young woman coming out—undoubtedly a model, Liz decided. She had that sleek look.

An idea popped into her head. "Hi," Liz said to her. "I wonder if you could help me."

"Well, I'll try," the young woman replied.

"You're a model, aren't you?"

"Yes, I am."

"Do you work for the agency in this building?"

"Yes, I do."

"I'm trying to locate two friends who are models and I think they worked for this agency too. They're twin sisters. I went to the condo where they used to live but they've moved and the neighbors didn't know where they've gone. I was on my way up to the agency to see if they knew, but perhaps you could tell me." The part about going to the condo and finding they'd moved was a last-minute inspiration. Pop would be proud of her, Liz thought with an inward smile.

"Twin models," the young woman said. "That sounds like Heather and Clover Prentiss."

"That's right. Do you know them?"

"Sure. I did a shoot with Clover a few weeks ago and a couple of shoots with Heather after that, but I haven't seen either of them since. I heard they moved to New York."

"New York!" Liz pretended to be surprised. "Well, I'm glad I ran into you before I wasted any more time looking for them in Fort Lauderdale."

"Sorry I couldn't have been more help, but I didn't know either of them very well. I never saw them except when we worked together. Talk around the agency was that they were very close and didn't go out of their way to make friends. I've heard twins are often like that." She looked at her watch. "I must run. I hope you locate them."

Liz found Mom in the gift shop and spent a little

while browsing with her before heading back to the car. She hoped when they got there Eichle would be gone.

He was still there. She made the best of the situation. "Mom, I don't think you've met Detective Eichle," she said. "He and Pop used to work together."

Mom smiled and extended her hand. "What a pleasant surprise for Frank, running into you down here."

"Nice to meet you, Mrs. Rooney," Eichle said. "And it was a pleasant surprise for me too. We've been reminiscing."

"Are you at Frank's old precinct?" Mom asked.

"Yes. I was just telling him we all miss him."

"Liz's best friend graduated from Police Academy a few months ago and she's at that precinct too," Mom said. "Maybe you know her—Sophie Pulaski?"

Liz wished she could disappear into a Florida sinkhole. Eichle would have to be pretty dense not to know Sophie had been feeding her information about the case. She didn't dare to look at him. She knew he must be fuming.

His voice was amazingly calm. "Yes, I know Sophie," he said. When she stole a glance at him she saw the look on his face she'd seen a dozen times before, only this time it was worse. He managed a smile for Mom and Pop. "Well, I know you want to get on with your house hunting," he said, "so I'll say 'so long.' It's been great seeing you again, Frank, and I'm glad to have met you, Mrs. Rooney."

As Mom and Pop said goodbye he turned to Liz, saying, "I'll see you back in New York." Then he turned and left.

NINE

"You've been awfully quiet all morning, Liz," Mom said, as they drove around a community of houses and condos. "Didn't you like any of the places we saw?"

Liz knew Mom was totally unaware of the concern caused by her remark to Eichle. Neither she nor Pop knew about the morsels of information Sophie came up with almost every day. Till this morning, only she and Sophie had known.

"I guess I'm overwhelmed," she replied. "They're all so nice. How are you ever going to decide?"

But now Eichle knew. He could make things difficult for Sophie. Maybe this would go on Sophie's record and interfere with her dream of being accepted into detective training. Liz considered herself responsible. She felt sick about it.

"I still like that place in Sarasota best," Pop said. "How about you, Marge?"

"Yes, that one gets my vote too," Mom replied.

"We'll go look at it again tomorrow, before we take Liz to the airport," Pop said.

Mom sighed. "I hate to think of her leaving already. It's been such a short visit. Couldn't you call Dan and ask if you could stay a little longer, Liz?"

"No way, Mom. He did me a huge favor letting me off for three days on such short notice."

Was there a regulation requiring police officers to keep what they heard in the squad room strictly confidential? Whether or not there was, she must phone Sophie and tell her Eichle knew about her eavesdropping. The damage had been done, but at least Sophie would be forewarned. When Eichle confronted her she wouldn't be taken by surprise. She'd phone Sophie as soon as they got to Sarasota tonight. Even if Eichle flew back to New York today, he wouldn't report to the precinct till tomorrow.

There was one bright spot in this bleak situation. Eichle knew Sophie hadn't given her Heather's name. Since the police were withholding this information, that would have been a serious offense. But Eichle would recall the encounter in the morgue. He'd remember that the ubiquitous Rooney had been there when Heather had introduced herself to Dan.

She wished she could discuss this with Pop, but now was not the time. He had enough to think about, trying to decide where he and Mom were going to live. She went to the park office to call Sophie. The mobile home didn't have a regular connection, and Pop said the cell phone picked up too much static on long distance. If Sophie wasn't home she'd leave a message with Mrs. Pulaski. Nothing as thought

provoking as *"Eichle's wise to the eavesdropping,"*
she decided. It would have to be something that
wouldn't arouse Mrs. Pulaski's curiosity.

Sophie wasn't home.

"You're not back already, are you, Liz?" Mrs.
Pulaski asked. "I thought you said tomorrow night."
When Liz told her she was still in Florida, Mrs.
Pulaski wanted to know how the folks were and
said be sure and give them her best regards. This
provided time to think of an innocuous message for
Sophie.

"Mrs. Pulaski. Would you please tell her I ran
into George in Florida and he was surprised to hear
we're close friends? I'll talk to her about it when I
get home."

Evidently the message didn't pique Mrs. Pulaski's
sense of intrigue. "Sure, Liz, I'll tell her," she said.

IMAGES OF EICHLE cornering Sophie with accusations
the next day kept Liz awake half that night.

"Are you okay, dear?" Mom asked, at breakfast.
"You don't look your usual bright-eyed self."

"Maybe she doesn't want to go back to the big
city," Pop said. "Maybe she'd rather stay down here
with us and live in one of those nice places we looked
at."

Liz laughed. "Don't tempt me."

"Well, you're going to be tempted this morning

when we take another look at that place we all liked," Pop said.

Liz knew he was joking. The last thing he and Mom wanted in their retirement life was the permanent presence of a grown daughter. "I'm afraid I'll have to settle for occasional visits," she said. "There aren't enough murders down here to keep me happy."

After they took another look at the area Mom and Pop liked best, they had lunch at a restaurant, and then it was time to go to the airport. At the gate, Mom got teary. "It seems like you just arrived and now you have to go," she said.

"Maybe when you come down again we'll be living in one of those nice houses we saw," Pop said.

WHEN SHE GOT TO HER apartment she found a message from Sophie. "Hi. It's me. Call me when you get in. I'll be home because Ralph's on duty tonight."

Sophie answered on the first ring. "Liz?"

"Yes, I just got in. Did you decipher my message?"

"Yes. Very clever. Imagine running into Eichle down there. So he knows we're best friends. That means he must be on to what we've been doing. How did he find out we know each other?"

Liz told her about Mom's innocent remark. "I could tell he was furious. Has he confronted you yet?"

"No. He's still on vacation. Rothman says he'll be back tomorrow."

"Good. You have more time to come up with a defense."

"Well, it isn't as if I've been giving away state secrets," Sophie replied.

Suddenly Liz remembered Sophie's visit to Ralph's family. "How did it go with Mama Perillo?" she asked.

Sophie's voice lightened. "It went great. Ralph's mother turned out to be a doll. She and his father and brothers made me feel right at home. I'll tell you all about it when I see you. Can you meet me after work tomorrow?"

"Sure," Liz replied. "I'll see you tomorrow at the newsstand." Sophie would have more to talk about tomorrow than her visit with Ralph's family, Liz thought. Eichle would be back, and despite Sophie's casual attitude, that meant trouble.

A few minutes after her call to Sophie, the phone rang. The Caller ID number wasn't familiar. She decided not to answer it. When the message came on she recognized Heather's voice. "I guess you're not home yet, Liz. I wish you were there. I need someone to talk to."

Liz grabbed the phone. "I'm here, Heather. What's on your mind?"

"Oh, Liz. I took your advice and phoned my boyfriend in Florida tonight."

"You did? What happened?"

"Well, at least he didn't hang up on me."

"Did you tell him you were going back to Fort Lauderdale?"

"Yes, I told him I didn't know exactly when, and he asked me if I had a lease on the apartment. I shouldn't have told him I'm renting month to month because then he wanted to know why I couldn't leave as soon as this month was up. I didn't want to tell him about Clover."

Of course the boyfriend wouldn't know about Clover, Liz thought. Although the Ormsby case had made the news all over the country, the sisters' names and the fact that they were twins had not been divulged. He had no idea that Heather was involved.

"So how did the conversation end?" she asked.

"He said I have to make up my mind and if I'm not back in Fort Lauderdale by the first of the month, it's over with us. Oh, Liz, I don't know what to do. I can't leave here yet, not knowing what happened to Clover."

"Maybe you should tell him about Clover. Then he'd understand."

"I can't tell him. I can't let him know Clover and I are the sisters involved in this murder case. Detective Eichle says he wants to keep us anonymous. He says if the news media finds out my name I'll be hounded day and night."

Didn't she trust her boyfriend to keep this confidential? Liz wondered.

"Talk to Detective Eichle about it," she said. "If he's having your name withheld solely out of consideration for you, I'm sure he'd say go ahead, tell your boyfriend."

Heather was silent for a moment. When she spoke, her voice seemed uncertain. "I don't know, Liz…"

She didn't want her boyfriend to know that her twin sister was a suspect in a sensational murder case, Liz thought. While that was understandable, if she really loved this guy she'd do it, and if he really loved her it wouldn't matter to him.

"Can we get together tomorrow?" Heather asked.

"I'll be tied up for a while after work, but we could get together after that. Do you want to meet somewhere for dinner?"

"I'd rather you came here for dinner."

"But you just had me over. I'd suggest you coming to my place, but I just got back, and tomorrow I won't have time to go grocery shopping."

"Please come to my place, Liz."

"Well, all right. But as soon as I get my fridge stocked it's my turn."

She hung up the phone thinking Heather sounded lonely and pathetic.

SOPHIE DIDN'T PHONE her at the office the next day. Eichle was back and he'd confronted her, she thought.

Sophie was steering clear of the phone except for incoming calls.

While waiting for Sophie at the newsstand, she bought a newspaper. For the first time, Ormsby's murder was off the front page, supplanted by a huge drug bust. A run-down of the poisoning case appeared on page three, along with a photo of Judson, a review of circumstances leading to his arrest, and his release on bail. Judson was in seclusion with relatives in Brooklyn awaiting his trial date, the article stated. No mention was made of the missing sister. As far as the news media was concerned, the concept of a mysterious brunet beauty slipping poison to the man who'd spurned her was defunct, she decided.

But not as far as Eichle was concerned, she thought. He'd gone to Fort Lauderdale for no other reason than to delve into Clover's past. He must have dug up plenty about her at the modeling agency. She wished she knew what.

Sophie arrived. "Sorry I'm late," she said.

Liz envisioned a showdown with Eichle just before quitting time. "What did he say?" she asked, as they walked to the coffee shop.

"You mean Eichle? Nothing. I got here late because Ma phoned just as I was leaving. She wanted to remind me to get home early. It's my father's birthday."

"But when Eichle came in this morning, he said something to you then, didn't he?"

Sophie shook her head. "He never said a word all day about me giving you information. If you hadn't told me he found out about it, I never would have suspected he knows. Are you sure he picked up on it, Liz?"

"I'm certain he did." There was no mistaking the cold look in his eyes, she thought, or his parting words, "I'll see you back in New York."

When they had settled themselves in a booth at the coffee shop, a disturbing thought flashed into her mind. Maybe he'd decided to leave Sophie alone and make trouble for *her,* instead. Maybe he'd contact Dan and insist she be excluded from any future homicide scenes. Maybe he'd lodge a formal complaint with the Commissioner.

Sophie started to tell her all about visiting Ralph's family. Liz didn't want to break into the happy dissertation. By the time each member of the Perillo family was described, along with how welcome they'd made her feel, Sophie said she had to leave. "I'll call you tomorrow," she said. "But I guess I'd better lighten up on the eavesdropping for a while."

It was clear Sophie didn't take the situation seriously, Liz thought. She wished she could be as casual about it. The thought that Eichle might zero in on *her* bothered her. She glanced at her watch. Time to get over to Heather's place.

TEN

WHEN LIZ PRESSED THE buzzer for Heather's apartment there was no response. She tried it again. Still no answer. She remembered she'd told Heather she'd be tied up for a while after work. Maybe Heather had gone out to the store. She'd probably be along in a few minutes.

She waited. The minutes passed with no sign of Heather. She pressed the buzzer again. Again no response. Could Heather be taking a nap and not hear the buzzer? She decided to try the superintendent's apartment and explain the situation. He'd let her into the building and she could ring Heather's doorbell and know. Surely that would rouse her.

She pushed the bell over *Manuel Delgado, Building Superintendent.* A woman's voice answered. "Yeah?"

"May I speak to Mr. Delgado?" she asked.

A sigh came over the wire. "He's not here. What's the problem? You lock yourself out?"

"No, I don't live here. One of the tenants is expecting me but she doesn't answer her buzzer. I think maybe she's asleep. I thought Mr. Delgado could let me in and I could knock on her door."

"You sure she's home?"

"I think so. She's expecting me for dinner."

"What's the tenant's name?"

"Prentiss. Apartment 2-A."

"Oh, the twin sisters. Yeah, one of them's home. I saw her come in with groceries about two o'clock this afternoon and she didn't go out again."

Mrs. Delgado kept close track of the tenants, Liz thought. "Since your husband's not there, could you let me in?" she asked.

"Yeah, but I'll have to go up there with you and make sure it's okay." A few moments later a fleshy, middle-aged woman with a cigarette dangling from her mouth opened the door.

"Mrs. Delgado?"

"Yeah, that's me," the woman said. She led Liz to the elevator and pressed the button.

"I appreciate you letting me in," Liz said.

"I wouldn't do it for everybody. We got to be careful, you know?" She glanced up at the indicator. Frowning, she gave the elevator button another jab. "We got to wait. Looks like 4-C's holding the door open again while he talks with 4-D."

She was well acquainted with the tenants and their habits, Liz thought. Had she picked up anything about Heather and Clover during the short time they'd lived here? Had she noticed Clover hadn't been around for the past week? With a few casual questions she'd find out. But she knew she must be careful. Mrs. Delgado must not get the slightest whiff of suspicion that the twin sisters who'd rented apartment 2-A were the same ones mentioned in the news media regarding the Ormsby case.

"You're sure you saw one of the sisters coming in with groceries this afternoon?" she asked.

"Yeah, but don't ask me which one. I only saw her through the window, and even close up it's hard to tell which is which."

"They're as alike as two peas in a pod," Liz said. Evidently Mrs. Delgado hadn't noticed Clover's absence during the past week.

"Yeah. The only way I can tell is one of them don't talk much. Hardly speaks to me. The other one— she's friendlier."

"She's the one who invited me for dinner," Liz said. On an impulse she added, "Her sister's been out of town for a few days."

Mrs. Delgado looked surprised. "Yeah? I could of sworn I saw her yesterday." At that moment a rumbling sound announced the arrival of the elevator. The door opened. An elderly man got off.

"Good evening, Mrs. Delgado," he said.

"Yeah, good evening, Mr. Kroner," Mrs. Delgado replied. "He's the one been holding us up," she whispered.

Liz breathed her silent thanks to Mr. Kroner. A quick trip up on the elevator would not have given her time for talk. She now knew that Clover was unfriendly and withdrawn. This might indicate she was in a depression. As for Mrs. Delgado being sure she'd seen Clover yesterday, that was impossible. Even if Clover were alive and in hiding, she couldn't hide in her own apartment, especially from Heather.

They stepped off the elevator. Mrs. Delgado rang Heather's bell, then rapped sharply on the door. "Miz Prentiss," she called. "You got company."

There was no response. She knocked again, this time with knuckle-bruising force. After a few moments, Liz heard footsteps and then Heather's voice, sounding foggy. "Is that you, Liz?"

"Yes. Are you all right, Heather?"

Heather opened the door. She *had* been asleep, Liz thought. Though she was fully clothed, she looked disheveled and groggy. "I'm sorry," she said. "I must have been out of it not to hear the buzzer. Thanks for letting her in, Mrs. Delgado."

"Okay," Mrs. Delgado said. Liz saw her cast Heather a sharp look before she turned to go.

Inside the apartment, Liz realized what the sharp look was about. Mrs. Delgado must have suspected Heather had been drinking before she fell asleep. She was right. On the floor next to the living room couch Liz counted five empty beer bottles. Another bottle, half-full, stood on the end table with the empty six-pack carton. Before she could think of something to say, Heather began to weep. "What must you think of me? I'm so ashamed of myself."

Liz tried to hide her shocked surprise with a casual remark. "So, you felt like having a beer and it got out of hand."

Heather nodded and blinked back her tears. "Besides being sick with worry about Clover, I've been all upset about my boyfriend in Florida saying if I'm not down there by the first of the month it's all off with us. When I got home from the store this afternoon I thought a beer would cheer me up."

"And it did, so you thought you'd have a couple more to feel even cheerier," Liz said, with a laugh.

The hint of a smile came to Heather's face. "Oh, Liz—you're so understanding. But here you are, expecting dinner, and I haven't even started cooking."

"Whatever you were planning to cook won't take long with the two of us pitching in."

"I was going to make spaghetti and garlic bread and a green salad."

"Unless you'd planned to make the sauce from scratch, we can have everything on the table in half an hour."

"From scratch? I'm not that good a cook. I buy the ready-made sauce and add stuff to it."

"Oh. I'm familiar with *that* recipe," Liz said. She glanced at Heather's red eyes and untidy appearance. "If you want to freshen up, I'll get things started."

"Thanks. I know I'm a mess. I'd like to take a shower and change clothes."

Liz nodded. "You'll feel much better after a shower."

Heather headed for her bedroom, saying, "The spaghetti and the sauce are in the cabinet over the stove. You'll find everything else in the fridge. I'll be out in a few minutes."

"Don't rush," Liz said. She wanted Heather to get back to normal. It was sad to see her in such a state.

She had things pretty well started when Heather called from the bedroom, "I'm out of the shower and you're right, I feel much better. I'll get dressed and be with you soon."

With the sauce simmering, the spaghetti bubbling and the garlic bread in the oven, there was nothing more to do except make the salad. She decided to set the table and leave the salad for Heather. She got cutlery and paper napkins from a kitchen drawer, but couldn't find any place mats. She remembered Heather had used place mats when she was here before. Maybe she kept them someplace in the living room. Sure enough, she found a stack of place mats in the top drawer of a chest near the kitchen door. She picked up two of them and was about to close the drawer when something caught her eye—a corner of a photograph protruding from under the pile of place mats. She pulled it out and looked at it. It was an enlarged photo of Heather and Clover, not as children or teenagers, but as they looked now.

She stared for a moment at the two pretty faces, identical even to their smiles, and the two willowy figures in identical poses. This had to be a recent shot, she thought. Their hairdos were fashionably current. They had on shorts and T-shirts. And judging from the palm trees in the background, the photo had been taken in Florida. A poignant thought struck her. This might be the last photo of them together, possibly just before they left for New York.

She closed the drawer. She wouldn't tell Heather she'd seen the photo, or ask why she hadn't shown it to her. After Clover's disappearance Heather must have put it away, she decided. It was probably too painful a reminder of happier days. Heather was having a rough enough time without being questioned about the photo. Heather's voice broke into her thoughts. "Oh, good, you found the place mats. And I see you have everything organized. Thanks so much, Liz."

She looked much better, Liz thought. "All we need is the salad and we're ready to eat," she said.

Heather took a bottle down from a cabinet. "We can't have spaghetti without Chianti," she said. "Will you open it while I'm making the salad? Wineglasses are on the shelf over the sink."

Liz couldn't help thinking if *she* had consumed almost an entire six-pack of imported beer and just awakened from an alcoholic stupor, she wouldn't even want to glimpse the label on a bottle of wine. Heather must have wonderful recuperative powers.

"Liz, you always cheer me up," Heather said, while they ate. "I don't know what I would have done if you hadn't come into my life. I'm going to miss you when I go back to Florida."

"Have you decided when you're going?"

"Not quite, but I'm thinking seriously about telling my boyfriend I have to give two weeks' notice about moving and I'll be down there after that."

"Have you given up on Clover coming back or being found?"

Heather's eyes saddened. "I don't think she's ever coming back, and I doubt that they'll ever find her."

She *had* given up, Liz thought. Maybe she'd decided, after all, that Clover had committed suicide and realized the body should have turned up by now, unless Clover had thrown herself into one of the rivers and been swept out to the ocean. *Or unless she was alive and in hiding.* Liz couldn't seem to let go of that possibility.

"I haven't told Detective Eichle I'm going back to Florida," Heather said. "But I'm sure he won't object. They've found the killer. My being here isn't necessary." Heather believed Eichle was only into the body search, Liz thought. She hadn't an inkling that he was continuing the investigation of Clover on his own.

"He could always contact you in Florida if he has anything to report," she said.

Heather nodded. "I want to go back as soon as possible. I realize now I never should have come up here. I'm thankful my boyfriend still wants me."

"I guess you'll be glad to get back to work again," Liz said.

"Yes. I would have gone to a modeling agency when we first got here, but Clover wasn't interested. All she wanted to do was try and contact that man. She really thought he was going to marry her."

Liz didn't ask why she hadn't gone to a modeling agency by herself. New York was crowded with gorgeous young women seeking modeling careers. The field was highly competitive. Most likely Heather knew it would be easier for beautiful twins to break in than an individual.

After eating they watched an old Fred Astaire and Ginger Rogers musical on TV, mostly singing and dancing and a light, predictable story line.

"Wouldn't it be great if life was really like that?" Heather said, when it was over. Liz detected a wistful note in her voice.

Liz left soon afterwards. "Take care of yourself, Heather," she said. "I'll call you soon about having dinner at my place." She was going to tell her not to cheer herself up with a six-pack again, but decided to let it go. Heather was embarrassed enough about it as it was.

As she hailed a cab in front of the building, she recalled the last time she'd had dinner with Heather and Eichle had dropped in. He'd picked up a lot of information about Clover since then, she thought, but her chances were zero of finding out what. From now on he and Rothman would be careful. Eichle hadn't said anything to Sophie, but she knew sooner or later he'd have plenty to say to *her*.

But actions spoke louder than words, she thought, just before she went to sleep. She didn't care if he hauled her over the coals and back again as long as he didn't find some way to keep her from going to murder scenes.

ELEVEN

THE NEXT MORNING LIZ expected Dan to come to her desk and tell her he couldn't take her along to homicide scenes or the morgue anymore. She imagined what he'd say: *"Sorry, Liz, but I got a complaint from the chief of police…"*

Though this didn't mean she couldn't continue to follow murder cases, it wouldn't be the same. She'd already lost Sophie's input. Now she was going to lose Dan's. Well, at least she still had this case to follow. Eichle couldn't take away what she'd already found out—especially about Clover.

He must have found out plenty himself while he was in Florida, she thought. Had he uncovered information regarding her mental state? Was it incriminating enough to be used as evidence? Would he let Judson's attorney know about it before Judson went to trial, or would he present it to the D.A.?

These thoughts helped her get through a jumpy morning. With every footstep she heard she was sure Dan had arrived to break the disheartening news. Noontime came with no sign of him. He was waiting till after lunch to tell her, she decided.

She'd been back from lunch for more than an hour

and he still hadn't appeared. Surely he'd received the complaint, she thought. Eichle had been back since yesterday morning. Here it was Friday afternoon. There'd been more than enough time for it to go through channels. Was Eichle playing a cat-and-mouse game with her? Was he going to keep her in this state of anxiety all weekend?

It was almost quitting time when Dan came to her desk. She braced herself for the inevitable. "Sorry we didn't get a chance to talk yesterday about your Florida trip, Lizzie," he said. "Did you enjoy yourself?"

"Yes, I did," she replied.

"How are your folks?"

"They're both fine."

"Are they thinking of settling down in Sarasota?"

"I believe they are." *Get to the point, Dan!*

He cast her a quizzical smile. "You seem preoccupied, Lizzie. What's on your mind?"

"Don't you have something to tell me?" she asked.

The puzzled look on his face suggested he didn't know what she was talking about. After a moment he nodded. "Oh, you mean the latest homicide. I thought you were too involved with the Ormsby case to be interested in a routine drug-related killing. There was no mystery in it. The victim's already been identified and the alleged killer's in custody."

Liz hadn't even heard about the drug-related killing. Murders of this sort had become so common that they didn't get much media coverage. "I wasn't referring to that," she replied.

"What, then?" he asked.

She told him everything. "I thought the order to keep me away from murder scenes and the morgue would have come through by now. Eichle must be holding up his complaint just to make me squirm," she concluded.

He gave a hearty laugh. "You can quit worrying your pretty little head about that. In the first place, I don't take orders from the police department, and in the second place, I don't think Eichle would do such a thing. You said he didn't reprimand your friend."

"His beef is with me, not Sophie."

"Come on, Lizzie, you're making too much of this. Sure he gets annoyed with you, but…"

"He gets a lot more than annoyed. If you could have seen him in Florida you'd know he was furious with me."

"You haven't passed along what Sophie told you, have you, or anything else you've found out?"

"I told Pop, and of course Mom was in on it too. With their police background I thought it would be okay."

"Sure. They know when to keep mum. I guess you and your father had a great time discussing the case."

"Oh, we certainly did." She would have told him

Pop agreed with her that the missing twin was guilty, but her phone rang at that moment.

"I'll see you Monday," Dan said, as he turned to leave.

Sophie was on the phone. "I didn't dare call you before now," she said. "I feel like when Eichle's not watching me, Rothman is. I'm off in a few minutes. Want to meet for coffee? I have something I want to run by you."

"About the case?"

"No, nothing like that."

"Can't you tell me over the phone?"

"I could, but I'd rather tell you face-to-face so I can see whether or not you go for it."

What was Sophie up to? she wondered, as she hung up the phone. There'd been no mention of meeting Ralph tonight. Maybe she was going to suggest going to a movie she wasn't sure they'd both want to see.

While waiting for Sophie she bought a tabloid. On the second page a follow-up article on the Ormsby case stated that Judson's trial would take place early in June. Again, she wondered about the information Eichle had picked up in Florida. Was it incriminating enough to be used as evidence against Clover? Would Judson be released on the strength of it?

Sophie arrived. They started walking to the coffee shop. "Well, even if Eichle hadn't found out about my eavesdropping, there's nothing about the Ormsby case to overhear anymore," she said. "With Judson waiting for his trial, things are at a standstill. Eichle and Rothman are on another case."

But Eichle hadn't let go of Clover yet, Liz thought. "You said you had something to discuss with me," she said. "Something you weren't sure I'd go for."

"What are you doing over the weekend?" Sophie asked.

Liz hadn't even thought about the weekend. "I don't know," she replied. "Since I broke off with Wade I haven't been in much of a social whirl."

"That's what I want to talk to you about," Sophie said, as they settled themselves at a table. "Ralph has this friend at his precinct. I met him once and he's awfully nice. We think you might like him."

"Sounds like you're playing matchmaker," Liz said.

"I swear we're not," Sophie replied. "We know you're at loose ends right now, and so is he. We thought the four of us could go out somewhere tomorrow night."

Sophie was holding back on something. Liz cast her a sharp glance. "What's the catch?"

"Well, this friend of Ralph's, he's sort of… *married*."

Liz laughed. "That's like a woman being sort of pregnant."

"Not really. He's been separated from his wife

for almost three months. They're talking about divorce."

"Talking about it doesn't exactly make him an eligible bachelor."

"I know, but he's such a nice guy, and he's so lonesome. What harm would there be if you went out with him? It's not as if you'd be alone with him. Ralph and I would be there. The four of us would have a good time together. Won't you please consider it?"

It had been several months since Liz had been out with anyone but Wade. She liked the idea of spending an evening with someone who wouldn't hassle her. "If Ralph thinks he's a nice guy then it's okay with me," she said.

The look on Sophie's face suggested she hadn't told her everything. "Now what?" Liz asked.

"So you're okay with Ralph bringing him around to meet you?"

"Sure. Where and when?"

Sophie glanced at her watch. "Here, and just about now," she said.

"What! You could have given me time to comb my hair and put on some lipstick."

"You always look okay. Besides, I was afraid if I told you too far ahead you'd change your mind."

Liz glanced towards the entrance to the coffee shop. "Well, even if I wanted to, it's too late now," she said. "They're here."

She appraised Ralph's friend as the two men approached the table. No wonder Ralph and Sophie thought they'd hit it off, she thought. The round, pleasant face beneath the shock of sandy hair had the map of Ireland all over it.

Ralph made the introduction. "Liz Rooney, meet Dennis Dugan."

"I'm delighted to meet you, Liz Rooney," Officer Dugan said. "Too bad St. Patrick's Day's over. I would have loved to celebrate with you."

He needn't think he was the only one who could dish out blarney. "It would have been a pleasure, Dennis Dugan," she replied.

She noticed Sophie and Ralph exchange pleased glances.

"I know the plan was for you two to meet tonight and the four of us go out tomorrow night," Ralph said. "But as long as we're all here now, why not go somewhere for dinner?"

"Do you think you could stand me two evenings in a row?" Dennis asked Liz.

"I'll try to grin and bear it," she replied. She knew she was going to enjoy his company.

They took a taxi to an Italian restaurant where Ralph and Sophie often ate. It had a small area for dancing. An old jukebox provided music. "It plays old platters that were popular when my folks were dating, and even some from my grandparents' era," Sophie said.

Since it was still early, the place was almost empty.

While they waited for their orders to be served, Dennis put some quarters in the jukebox. A few moments later a tune from the big-band era came on. Liz recognized it right away. She'd grown up listening to Grandma McGowan's albums from the 1930's and 40's. "That's Glenn Miller's 'String of Pearls,' isn't it?" she asked.

"It is," he replied. "May I have the honor of this dance, Miss Rooney?"

"You may, Mr. Dugan." After weeks of uptight evenings with Wade, this was a welcome change.

On the dance floor he looked at her with a smile. "Thanks, Liz."

"Thanks for what?"

"For agreeing to meet me and go out with me. I know Sophie clued you in on my marital status."

"Yes, she did. I'm sorry you're having trouble. How long have you been married?"

"Two and a half years."

"Any kids?"

"No, and with the marriage going sour it's just as well."

"If you want to talk about it, I'm a good listener."

"There's not much to tell except Amy wants me to leave the force."

"She wouldn't be the only woman who couldn't hack being a cop's wife."

"It's not as if she didn't know what she was getting into. I was a cop when we met."

As a cop's daughter, Liz knew only too well what might make a police officer's wife want her husband to turn in his badge. She'd never forget one terrible night when she was a child. Pop's partner had been killed in the line of duty and Pop wounded. If Mom had wanted Pop to resign after that, she'd kept her feelings to herself. She'd heard Pop say over and over again that Mom was an ideal wife for a cop.

"What happened to make your wife want you off the force?" she asked.

"How did you know something happened?" he asked.

"My father's a retired cop."

"Then you know what can happen. In our case it was the husband of Amy's best friend, shot and killed while trying to break up a fight between two punks. Besides his wife, he left two kids, one of them only four months old." He paused. "I shouldn't be laying all this on you. Some fun date I turned out to be."

She sensed he was hurting. His lighthearted manner and blarney were cover-ups. "You're deeply in love with your wife, aren't you?" she asked.

"Yes," he replied, without hesitation. "She loves me too, but she says if I don't quit being a cop she's going to get a divorce." He glanced towards the table. "Looks like our food's being served." On the way back to the table he said, "I promise I won't talk about my troubles anymore."

"If you change your mind, I'll listen," she replied.

As they sat down, Ralph suggested they have dinner somewhere in the city the following evening and take in a show at Radio City Music Hall. They all agreed. Then Dennis resumed his wit and blarney and kept them laughing throughout the meal. It wasn't until they left the restaurant that he mentioned his wife again.

As they stood on the sidewalk looking for a cab, he glanced at Liz with a rueful smile. "I said I'd stop talking about Amy's ultimatum, but may I ask you something?"

With Sophie and Ralph engrossed in their own talk and no cab in sight, this was a good time for him to confide in her again, Liz thought. "Sure, go ahead," she said.

"From a woman's standpoint, do you think there's any hope for my marriage?"

Liz pondered this. If she were in love with a good man and faced with the same situation, she wouldn't give him up before making every effort to work something out. "Yes, there's hope. You need to talk this through and make a compromise."

"How can we do that when all Amy wants is for me to quit being a cop and I never wanted to be anything else but a cop?"

Liz thought of the dreadful night when Pop lost his partner and she and Mom almost lost Pop. "Amy's afraid of the risks a New York cop faces," she said. "If you were willing to relocate somewhere away from New York—maybe to a small town where the crime rate is low—maybe then she'd reconsider."

He was silent for a moment before nodding his head. "I hadn't thought of that," he said. "I wouldn't mind being on a small-town police force. I think there's a chance Amy will go for it." He smiled. "Thanks, Liz. I owe you one."

"Here comes a taxi," Ralph said.

When they dropped Liz off at her apartment, Dennis thanked her again. "Soon as I get home I'm going to phone Amy and run your idea past her. I'll let you know her reaction when I see you tomorrow night."

Only a foolish, self-centered woman wouldn't be willing to meet a man like Dennis Dugan halfway, Liz thought, as she entered her apartment. She thought of Wade. He'd never have suggested that they compromise on her "morbid interest in murders." But suppose he had. She imagined him laying down the rules: *"I'll allow you to follow one homicide per year, but only if Mother approves."*

She checked her answering machine. There was one message and Heather's number was displayed on the caller ID. She'd called at half past seven. She listened to the message. Heather sounded petulant, she thought. "Liz, you promised you'd phone me about having dinner again. If it's not too late when you get home, please call me."

As if she'd been waiting by the phone, Heather picked up on the first ring. "Is that you, Liz?"

"Yes, I just got in."

"Where were you?"

"I had dinner with some friends."

"You said we were going to have dinner together tonight. You were going to call me about it, remember?"

"I remember I said I'd call you, but I didn't say anything about tonight."

"Yes, you did. I've been waiting for your call ever since you were here."

Liz's annoyance at being put on the defensive gave way to compassion. Heather was worried about Clover and starved for companionship. "Well, let's set something up," she said. "How about having brunch somewhere tomorrow? Afterwards we could take in an art exhibit at one of the museums or we could go to a movie or the zoo."

"Instead of brunch tomorrow, couldn't we have dinner at your place like we discussed before?"

"I'm sorry. I have something else on for tomorrow night."

Heather didn't reply. For a moment Liz thought she'd hung up. "Are you still there, Heather?" she asked.

"Yes. I'm here. I understand you have other friends you want to be with, but I'm disappointed."

Her voice sounded very sad, Liz thought. She'd thought about going to visit Grandma McGowan on Sunday, but she could go early and make it back to Manhattan in time for dinner with Heather. "How about Sunday night?" she asked. "I'll fix us a good dinner and we can have a nice visit."

"Okay." Heather still sounded downcast. "But I'd counted on getting together tomorrow night. I get so lonesome without Clover and you always cheer me up."

Liz knew she had no reason to feel guilty, but she couldn't help it. "Tell you what," she said. "I could drop by your place tomorrow afternoon for a while. Okay?" She'd visit with Heather for a couple of hours before meeting Sophie, Ralph, and Dennis at the restaurant, she decided.

"A little while is better than nothing," Heather said. "What time will you be here?"

"Is four o'clock okay?"

"Yes…I'll see you at four tomorrow."

Liz thought Heather still sounded disappointed about not having dinner together tomorrow night. Maybe the visit tomorrow afternoon would perk her up.

TWELVE

LIZ WAS JUST FINISHING breakfast the next morning
when Sophie phoned. "I'm calling from work," she
said. "Rothman's off this Saturday and Eichle's away
from his desk so the coast is clear. Not that I have
anything to tell you about the Ormsby case, anyway.
Nobody around here even mentions it anymore."

Was Eichle still pursuing it? Liz wondered. She
didn't have time to ponder this. Sophie hadn't stopped
talking, though she'd changed the subject.

"You made a hit with Dennis. After we dropped
you off last night he told us you really cheered him
up."

"All I did was play Dear Abby. He asked for advice
and I made a suggestion."

"Did you give him some advice about his marriage
problem?"

"He confided in me, Sophie. I don't think I should
talk about what either of us said."

"He already told Ralph and me about his wife
insisting he leave the force, but you're right, I guess
what you told him should remain confidential unless
he brings it up. Maybe he will, tonight. Whatever

advice you gave him, I hope it works. Ralph says his wife is very nice."

Nice enough to make a compromise, Liz hoped. Suddenly she remembered her promise to Heather. "I have to drop in on Heather for a little while before I meet you tonight," she said. "She lives on Forty-first Street, and I'll take a cab from there. I'll give myself plenty of time, but in case I get stuck in traffic I won't be more than a few minutes late."

"Are you still digging for something about Clover?"

"I'm always on the alert for something every time I'm with Heather, but I'm going over there tonight because she sounded awfully lonely when I talked to her on the phone. I want to try and cheer her up."

"I know you're good at that," Sophie said. She lowered her voice. "I gotta go. Eichle's back."

"See you tonight at six," Liz replied.

She glanced at her watch. Time for a TV news and weather report. She didn't expect there'd be anything about the Ormsby case, but she wanted to hear what kind of an evening was forecast so she'd know what to wear. Late March could be blustery and cold, or it could be mild.

According to the weatherwoman, it was going to be a nice evening, with temperatures in the low sixties. Good, she thought, she could wear a pantsuit or a skirt and blazer and forget a topcoat.

The news came on. She didn't need to watch,

she'd just listen, she thought. She started to wash her breakfast dishes, when she heard the newscaster mention the Ormsby case. A moment later she was startled to hear him mention a familiar name: *Cherie La Salle.*

She rushed out from behind the screen just in time to see a photo of the glamorous Cherie wearing the skimpy, feathered costume she'd worn in her last Broadway musical. The newscaster went on to say Cherie was suing the estate of Theodore Van Brunt Ormsby. Her attorney was quoted as stating that, as Ormsby's fiancée, she was entitled to a portion of his wealth.

"Miss La Salle is only asking for a fair amount, nowhere near what she'd be entitled to had the marriage taken place," he stated. He went on to say the wedding had been planned for the coming August and he explained that Cherie had been too overcome with grief to say anything about it till now.

And now she was out to get whatever she could, Liz thought. Just as she asked herself if it could be true and the notorious playboy had decided to settle down, the newscaster made another statement. An investigative reporter had been contacted by an employee of the prestigious Manhattan jewelry firm, Cartier's, whose dazzling gems had graced the fingers, ears, necks, and bosoms of wealthy socialites since the nineteenth century. This employee disclosed that several weeks ago Mr. Theodore Van Brunt

Ormsby had ordered a flawless, three-carat diamond fashioned into a platinum ring and engraved it with the tender sentiment, *C and T forever.*

Liz could scarcely believe her ears. After the newscaster had gone on to other items she turned this over in her mind. Had Cherie known about the ring? If so, why hadn't she said something about it herself, instead of having it dug up by a reporter? Perhaps she was telling the truth when she said she'd been too grief-stricken. Liz recalled the tabloids saying she'd been in seclusion since the murder. Well, whatever the reason, there was no doubt she was Ormsby's fiancée.

She kept the TV on in case more news came on about Cherie. Throughout the morning and early afternoon the subject was repeated on other news programs but there were no new twists. She and Sophie would have a lot to talk about tonight, she thought.

At quarter to four she left for Heather's place. She took the subway and got to Heather's building shortly after four.

Heather answered her ring at the building's entrance. "Is that you, Liz?"

Her voice sounded strange, Liz thought. She hoped Heather hadn't been drinking again. "Yes, it's Liz," she replied.

Heather buzzed her in. It was only one flight up, so she took the stairs instead of the elevator. She rang Heather's doorbell and heard the key turn in the dead bolt. Heather opened the door. Liz thought she looked distraught.

"I wasn't sure you'd come," she said.

"I told you I'd be here, didn't I?" Liz asked, as she followed Heather into the foyer.

Heather looked at her with a frown. "Yes, but you also told me you'd call me about us having dinner together tonight, and instead you made other plans."

"Oh, come on, Heather. You know that was a misunderstanding."

"Whatever it was, I felt betrayed," Heather said. Liz stared at her, too surprised to reply. Before she could think of something to say, Heather changed the subject. "Have you heard the news today or read the afternoon newspapers?" she asked.

Liz guessed she'd heard about Cherie's lawsuit and the diamond engagement ring. This must be what got her so upset, she decided. "Yes, I heard about Cherie La Salle's engagement to Ormsby," she said.

Heather began to weep. "She has no right to call herself his fiancée. That ring was ordered for Clover," she sobbed. "She was the 'C' in the engraving, not her. He must have ordered the ring right after he got back from Florida, but that woman got him in her clutches somehow. She has something on him. She was probably blackmailing him. It was Clover he really loved and wanted to marry."

Liz listened in silence to the irrational ranting. There would be no sense in trying to reason with

Heather. She was too distraught. "Heather, I think some hot tea would do us both good," she said. "You sit down and relax. I'll put the kettle on and…"

Heather interrupted. "I don't want tea. What I need is a good stiff drink."

Liz decided not to argue with her. "Do you have any brandy? I've heard tea laced with brandy is very soothing." She could put a very small amount in the teapot, she thought.

"I don't have any brandy, but there's a bottle of bourbon in the cabinet over the refrigerator," Heather replied.

"I guess bourbon would be just as good," Liz said. She headed for the kitchen, saying, "Now you just relax. I'll set a tray and bring everything in."

"Thank you," Heather said.

Maybe she'd been forgiven for the "betrayal," Liz thought, as she put the kettle on. When she started to arrange the tea tray she decided it needed something to keep the teapot and cups and saucers from sliding. A place mat would do. She remembered Heather kept them in the top drawer of that chest outside the kitchen door. As she opened the drawer and picked up a place mat, she recalled the photo of Heather and Clover she'd seen when she was here before. She looked under the place mats. It was still there. She took it out and gave it a fleeting glance, wondering, again, why Heather hadn't shown it to her.

"Did you find everything you need?" Heather called from the couch.

Liz quickly replaced the photo and closed the drawer. "Yes. Tea's almost ready. I'll bring the tray in a few minutes."

"Bring the bourbon too," Heather said.

So much for the plan to sprinkle a few drops into the teapot, Liz thought. She carried the tray into the living room, placed it on a table near the sofa, and poured the tea into their cups.

Heather eyed the sugar bowl and milk pitcher. "You needn't have brought those in," she said. "They wouldn't set well with bourbon."

"I guess I put them on the tray without thinking," Liz replied.

Heather picked up the bottle. "Pass your cup."

"Oh, I put some in my cup while I was in the kitchen," Liz said. The lie was justified. If Heather was going to drown her sorrows, she had to keep her wits about her.

Heather poured a generous amount of bourbon into her tea and took a swallow. "Mmm, this is good," she said.

"Delicious," Liz said. Another lie. She didn't enjoy tea without a splash of milk and a little sugar.

Heather didn't sip her tea. She drained her cup in a couple of quaffs. "I'm ready for a refill," she announced. This round she added at least two ounces of bourbon.

After the second cup, Heather perked up. She seemed to have temporarily forgotten Cherie La Salle and the ring she claimed was meant for Clover. They started swapping funny stories about their childhoods and their adolescent years. It disturbed Liz when Heather put more bourbon in her third cup of tea, but there was nothing she could do to stop her.

Suddenly, as if a button had been pressed or a switch turned, Heather's mood changed. "I suppose you'll be telling me you have to leave in a few minutes," she said.

"Well, I do," Liz replied. "I'm meeting my friends at a restaurant at six."

"Why did you make plans with them after you told me we were going to have dinner together tonight?" Heather asked.

Liz sighed. "We've been over that. I told you I'd phone you. I never mentioned a specific night."

"Yes, you did. I distinctly remember you said Saturday."

Liz rose from the sofa. "I'm sorry, but you misunderstood." She picked up the tea tray. "I'll clear these dishes away and then I must go. I don't want to keep my friends waiting."

"It wasn't a misunderstanding," Heather insisted.

Liz took the tray, bottle and all, into the kitchen. Maybe by the time she washed the dishes Heather's mood would have mellowed. When she returned to the living room, she noticed a strange smile on

Heather's face. "Your friends are going to have a long wait," she said.

"What do you mean by that, Heather?"

"I mean I locked the dead bolt on the apartment door and hid the key."

"You're kidding, of course," Liz said.

Heather shook her head. "This is no joke. Clover and I have both been betrayed by someone we trusted. Poor Clover can't get even, but I can. I'm going to keep you here until your friends feel as betrayed as I do—until they feel they can't trust you."

This can't be happening, Liz thought. She tried to steady her voice. "You don't want to do this, Heather. Get the key and unlock the door and we'll forget about it."

Heather only looked at her with that strange smile and shook her head.

Liz's mind went into high gear. Mrs. Delgado lived in the apartment directly below this one. Maybe, if she went into the bathroom and stomped on the floor or banged on the plumbing, she'd come up to find out what all the nose was about. But then anther thought flashed into her mind.

"My friends know I stopped here on my way to meet them. They know your name. When they've waited for ten or fifteen minutes they'll phone here to see if I've left yet."

"They won't find my name in the phone book,"

Heather replied. "We haven't lived here long enough to be listed."

"They know you live on Forty-first Street. They'll get your number from information."

"It's going to be an unlisted number anyway," Heather retorted. "Information won't give it to them."

Liz began to lose patience. "Now you listen to me, Heather," she said. "My friends are all cops. They can get your number from the phone company whether it's unlisted or not."

Heather's eyes widened. She looked uncertain. "You're bluffing," she said.

"Do you want to wait and see if I'm bluffing?" Liz asked.

"If they call I won't answer the phone," Heather said.

Liz gave a knowing smile. "Cops are naturally suspicious. Do you want them to come here looking for me? The phone company will give them your exact address."

Heather hesitated. "Well, if they call I'll answer the phone and say you're not here—you never showed up."

Liz managed a wry laugh. "Not if I grab the phone first."

Heather remained defiant. "I'll get the phone away from you."

Liz deliberately let a long glance sweep over Heather's delicate, model-slim form. "Don't count on it," she said. "You wouldn't stand a chance against a scrappy, redheaded mick. Now unlock that door—unless you'd rather be thrown in jail for keeping me here against my will."

Heather began to weep. "I only wanted to teach you a lesson."

"Just unlock the door, Heather," Liz said.

Still sobbing, Heather lifted up a vase on the table and produced the key. Without a word, she went out into the foyer. Liz followed her, still not sure she'd actually unlock the door, but she did. Liz was out of the apartment in a split second. "Well, so long, Heather," she said.

Heather's eyes still streamed with tears. "You hate me now, don't you?"

"No, I don't hate you, Heather, but you've got to get hold of yourself," Liz replied.

"You don't want me to have dinner with you tomorrow night, do you?"

"I think we'd better skip that."

"Do you ever want to see me again? Will you ever phone me again?"

"I don't know," Liz said. "We'll see." A moment later, she reconsidered. She was Heather's only friend and it was a case of too much bourbon in the tea. "Sure, I'll phone you again soon, Heather," she said. "But remember, I didn't mention a specific day."

It wasn't until she was in the taxi on her way uptown that the enormity of this experience struck her. Heather had been out of control. She actually would have held her there under lock and key, to "teach her a lesson." Even though the bourbon had caused Heather's irrational behavior, something like this could happen again, she thought. She told herself tonight was the last time she'd ever set foot in Heather's apartment.

When the cab turned into Rockefeller Center, she debated whether or not to mention the incident tonight. Sophie alone knew about her involvement with Heather. She said she hadn't told Ralph. Dennis certainly wouldn't be aware of it. There'd be no point in describing Heather's strange behavior. She could tell Sophie about it some other time, maybe tomorrow. Tonight she'd just try and forget it and enjoy herself.

"Sorry I'm late," she said, as she joined them in the lobby of the restaurant.

"Only a couple of minutes," Ralph said.

"That's pretty good, considering Saturday night traffic," Dennis added.

Sophie cast her a penetrating stare. "Are you okay, Liz?" she asked.

"Sure, why wouldn't I be?" Liz replied. But she knew she couldn't fool Sophie. They'd known each other too long. They were familiar with one another's every tone of voice, facial expression, and mannerism, and the moods that lay behind them. On the way to their table she whispered to Sophie, "Something happened. I'll tell you when we're alone."

She should have known better than to try and keep Sophie in suspense. As soon as they were seated, Sophie asked, "So how did it go with Heather?"

Liz looked at her with a slight frown. The frown was supposed to tell her to button her lip. Ralph and Dennis both picked up on her reluctance to talk about Heather. "Is Heather the friend you stopped to see on your way here?" Dennis asked.

She nodded and tried to think of some way to change the subject. But Ralph had already turned to Sophie. "Isn't Heather the name of the woman whose sister was a suspect in the Ormsby poisoning? Is this the same woman?"

Sophie had to admit it was.

"Is she a friend of yours, Liz?" Dennis asked.

"Not a close friend, but, yes, we're acquainted," Liz replied. She picked up a menu and pretended to scan the list of entrees. An item suddenly came into focus. "Oh, the poached salmon sounds good," she said.

"How come you don't want to talk about her?" Dennis asked.

The hazards of socializing with cops, Liz thought. She knew Dennis and Ralph had sensed something and they wouldn't let go till they knew what it was. "All right, I might as well tell you what happened," she said. "But it's kind of a long story. Let's order first."

While waiting for their food they all listened. She spared no detail. When she finished, Sophie was wide-eyed and open-mouthed. Dennis and Ralph looked both startled and serious.

"I'm no shrink, but the way this woman went on about being betrayed I'd say she's paranoid," Ralph said.

Dennis nodded. "You were lucky to get out of there in one piece."

"Oh, Heather wouldn't have harmed me. She's not a violent person," Liz said. "She didn't threaten me except to say she was going to keep me locked up for a while to teach me a lesson. I'm sure it was the bourbon in the tea that set her off."

"A little more bourbon and she might have turned violent," Ralph said.

"You should report this," Dennis advised.

Liz shook her head. "Oh, no. She's been through enough. I'll just let it go."

"You'd better let Heather go too," Sophie said.

"I suppose I should, but I'm the only friend she has in New York, and she's been so lonely without her sister. She told me they were very close."

"Well, don't go to her apartment anymore," Ralph said. "If you must continue to see her, have her over to your place. That way you can control the booze."

"I heard a rumor at the precinct—you probably

heard it too, Ralph—that this woman, Heather, and her missing sister are identical twins," Dennis said. He looked first at Sophie, then at Liz. "Anything to that?" When neither of them answered, he laughed. "I get it. This Heather's identity is being protected."

"I heard that story too," Ralph said. "If they are twins, that would make the case even more interesting."

"Since Judson's arrest, Heather and her missing sister don't figure in the case anymore," Sophie said.

"The case won't be closed till the trial is over," Dennis reminded her.

"There's still time for the houseman's attorney to dig up evidence against the missing sister," Ralph said.

Dennis looked around the table at each of them. "Do you mind if we get off the Ormsby case for a few minutes?" he asked. "I have some good news."

They all nodded. "Sure, let's hear it," Liz said.

He smiled around the table. "I phoned Amy last night and she didn't turn down my idea of relocating to a low-crime area. She said she'd think about it. I have a good feeling about this. I think she's going to say okay."

"Great!" Ralph said. "How did you come up with that idea?"

"A certain red-haired colleen suggested it," Dennis said, with a grin at Liz. From that moment the evening took on the nature of a celebration. Sparkling wine was ordered. Glasses were raised. Toasts were made to happy days ahead for Dennis and his wife.

It had been the best Saturday night she'd had in months, Liz thought, after they dropped her off at her apartment. As she prepared for bed, she tried to concentrate on the good time she'd had, but thoughts of Heather's behavior kept crowding her mind. After she turned out her light she found herself reviewing the entire episode. While recalling the brief interlude when she and Heather had a pleasant talk, she realized Heather hadn't mentioned her boyfriend or going back to Florida even once. Strange, she thought. Two days ago she could talk of little else. And something else was strange—the photo under the place mats. Why hadn't Heather shown it to her? She'd said the recent photos were still packed in the boxes, but she'd said she'd get some out and show them to her. That photo in the drawer must have been a recent one. The palm trees indicated it had been taken in Florida. Had Heather meant to show it to her and forgotten?

She fell asleep before she could think of an answer.

THIRTEEN

SINCE HER SUNDAY dinner with Heather was off, the next morning Liz followed through on her original plan to visit Grandma McGowan. She phoned Grandma right after breakfast to make sure she wasn't going off on a bus trip somewhere.

"I'm free after mass, until about two when I'm going to see a movie with a friend," Grandma said. "Come around half past eleven. We'll have lunch. It will be so nice to see you, dear."

She'd just finished talking to Grandma when Sophie called. Excitement sounded in her voice. "Liz! Guess what?"

"Your rich uncle died and left you a potful?"

"Better than that. Ralph and I are engaged."

"That's great! Congratulations! I guess you didn't know about this when we were together last night."

"Are you kidding? I couldn't have kept it to myself. It happened when Ralph brought me home last night. He said he was sick of making the trip all the way to Staten Island after every date and it would be much more convenient if I moved into his apartment, and then he said he knew a nice Polish girl wouldn't do that without a wedding ring on her finger, and I said, 'You got that right, Buster.'"

Liz laughed. "That's the most romantic marriage proposal and acceptance I ever heard. So you're going to take the plunge. Any idea when?"

"Probably the first Sunday in October. Oh, Liz, I'm so happy I feel delirious."

"Are you both off duty today so you can enjoy your delirious state together?"

"I am, but Ralph isn't. I won't be able to see him till tonight."

"I'm going to be on the island visiting my grand-mother today…"

"You are? Could you come over afterwards?"

"Sure. She has a movie date at two."

"Great. We'll have plenty of time to talk. See you around two."

Liz hoped Sophie would take some time out from her euphoria to discuss the Ormsby case. She wanted to review it, get all her facts and ideas organized, and see how they added up. She also wanted to tell Sophie about the photo hidden under the place mats. Too bad she hadn't been able to take a good look at it. Her fleeting glance had stirred something in her mind. She couldn't put her finger on it, but it was there every time she thought about the photo.

In the ferry terminal, she bought a Sunday *News*. Again, a picture of Cherie La Salle occupied most of the front page. This time she was wearing a fringed costume.

Cartier To Cherie—No Ring, the headline screamed. Text on the inside page stated that a spokesman for the prestigious jewelry firm had announced no order for a diamond ring was ever placed by Theodore Van Brunt Ormsby. The employee who'd given this false information to the press had been fired and could not be reached for comment. He must have craved the notoriety, however fleeting, Liz thought. Well, he'd had his fifteen minutes of fame. As for Cherie, she couldn't be reached for comment, either.

On the ferry, Liz thought over this new development. Heather must have heard about it by now. How had she reacted?

At the Staten Island ferry terminal she boarded the rapid transit train to the New Dorp station and walked the two blocks to the tree-lined street where Grandma lived. She passed the parochial school she and Sophie had attended from kindergarten till high school. These streets were crowded with memories. She recalled going to Grandma's house after school. There she'd have milk and cookies while waiting for Mom to pick her up. Mom had been a grade-school teacher in a public school in Port Richmond.

The house where they'd lived till Pop retired was only a short drive from Grandma's. Grandma lived within walking distance of Sophie's home. New Dorp had a nice, neighborly aura about it. Suddenly she wished she hadn't moved to Manhattan. She could have rented an apartment here or she could have moved in with Grandma. Grandma must be lonely since Grandpa died. Either way, she and Sophie could have taken the train and the ferry to work together, every day.

The nostalgia began to fade. Grandma wasn't lonely. She had a life of her own. The last thing she needed was a granddaughter living with her. As for Sophie, she'd soon be married and would probably go to live off the island. Whoever said, *"You can't go home again"* knew what he was talking about.

Having lunch in Grandma's kitchen was another reminder of bygone days, especially when Grandma hadn't changed much over the years. She wore a dress only one size larger, and she went to the beauty salon regularly to keep the gray out of her auburn hair.

Grandma knew about her interest in murder cases. "I know you've been following that billionaire playboy poisoning," she said, pouring tea into Liz's cup from the familiar old blue-and-white teapot. "How about that blond golddigger claiming she was engaged to him? Did you hear on the news the jeweler says no ring was ever ordered for her? If you ask me, she was in cahoots with the employee. They were going to split whatever she got from the estate, though it beats me how they thought they could get away with it."

Far out as Grandma's theory might sound, it was no crazier than Judson being indicted and the missing twin forgotten, Liz thought. Discussing a murder case with Grandma was another throwback. Over the years they'd talked about many. Liz suspected she'd inherited more than her red hair from Grandma McGowan.

"Who do you think did it, Gram?" she asked.

Grandma stirred her tea. "Not that man they arrested, that's for sure. If your father had been on the case it never would have happened. He'd have followed up on the woman who was in the penthouse and reported missing by her sister."

Liz liked getting Grandma's slant on the case. It seemed to agree with hers. "Do you believe the missing sister did it?" she asked. She was careful not to say "twin."

"Absolutely. Why would she have disappeared right after the poisoning if she didn't do it? But I think there's a lot more to this than meets the eye."

How right she was, Liz thought. She wanted to tell her the sisters were twins, but as long as the police wanted Heather's privacy protected, she mustn't. She'd only told Pop and of course Mom knew, but they understood the rules. She wasn't sure about Grandma. If she told her, it might be all over the island in a couple of days.

"Your mother wrote me you visited them in Florida," Grandma said. "She said they've almost decided to buy a place in Sarasota and they want me to visit them this winter."

"Yes, I got a few days off and flew down," Liz replied. "They showed me all the places they were considering. I saw the model of the house they like. You'd like it too, Gram. It has plenty of room for you to visit."

"It would be nice to get away from the cold for a week or so," Grandma said. They talked about Florida for a while before Grandma inquired about Sophie. "How is she? How does she like being on the force?"

"Sophie's fine. She likes being a cop, even though she's doing mostly clerical work right now. She hopes to be assigned to Patrol soon and eventually she wants to be a homicide detective."

"Last time I saw Mrs. Pulaski she told me Sophie was dating a cop and she thought it might be serious."

"I was just about to tell you, they're engaged and going to be married in October."

"That's nice…" Grandma cast her an inquisitive glance. "Are you still seeing the stockbroker?"

"Wade? No, we broke up a week or so ago." She laughed. "But before you ask me if there's anyone else in the picture, there isn't. However, if something should develop I'll let you know right away."

"Make sure you do," Grandma replied. She looked up at the clock over the refrigerator. "Oh, I've lost track of the time. I have to get ready for my movie date."

"A *date,* Gram?"

"Don't get any ideas. He's just a nice man I know from church. His wife died a couple of years ago and we get together now and then for dinner or a movie."

"I told Sophie I'd stop in after my visit here, so I'll be on my way," Liz said. A fine thing when your grandmother has a boyfriend but you don't, she thought with a chuckle.

SOPHIE WAS FULL of talk about her engagement. Ralph's mother had called her that morning to say Ralph had phoned to tell her the news and she was very happy about it and was having his grandmother's diamond ring reset for her. Curled up on the bed in her room, as they'd done since grade-school days, she talked nonstop before suddenly saying, "I haven't given you a chance to say a word, have I?"

"Well, no, but I'll say it now. I'm very happy for you and Ralph."

"But I'll bet you wouldn't mind if I changed the subject. Let's talk about the Ormsby case. Of course you heard Cherie's diamond engagement ring was a hoax."

"Yes, and I'm wondering how Heather will react to that. It was the ring thing that got her all bent out of shape last night."

"Maybe this will straighten her out. But whatever happens, I hope you'll take Ralph's advice and stay away from her apartment," Sophie said.

Liz suddenly remembered she wanted to tell Sophie about the photo in the place-mat drawer. "Here's something strange," she said. "The first time I went to Heather's place I saw a picture of her with Clover when they were little kids. They were dressed exactly alike. Heather told me their mother always dressed them in twin outfits but when they got older they refused to do it anymore. When I asked her if she had any recent photos of the two of them she said she did but they were still packed away. She said she'd try and find them and show them to me the next time I came."

"So what's strange about that?" Sophie asked.

"The next time I was there I offered to set the table and was looking for place mats and I found a stack of them in the top drawer of a chest, and underneath, like it had been deliberately hidden, was a photo of Heather and Clover all grown up."

"That is strange. Why didn't she show it to you? Do you think she might have meant to show it to you but forgot? Didn't you ask her about it?"

"No, I was going to, but then I didn't want her to think I'd been snooping."

Sophie laughed. "You, *snooping?*"

"Honest—this time I wasn't. I came across the photo quite by accident."

"Did you get a good look at it?"

"Only enough to know it was Clover and Heather and there were palm trees in the background. I saw it again when I was there last night and I would have asked her about it if she hadn't been drinking and acting strange. Since then I haven't been able to get that photo out of my mind. There was something about it. Maybe if I could look at it again carefully…"

"I hope you're not planning to go back there for another look at it."

"No way! Maybe if I think hard about the photo, whatever's bugging me about it will come to me."

LIZ CAUGHT THE 5:30 ferry back to Manhattan. When she checked her phone messages she found only one—from Heather. "Please call me when you get in, Liz." Her voice sounded perfectly normal. Evidently she hadn't been drinking, nor had the news about the Cartier diamond ring upset her. She decided to return the call. If she didn't, Heather would only call again.

Heather picked up promptly. Again, her voice sounded controlled. "Thanks for calling back, Liz," she said. "I wanted to tell you my boyfriend phoned me today and he's being much more reasonable about me returning to Florida. He's willing to wait awhile."

"I'm glad to hear that," Liz said. Yesterday it was

as if the boyfriend-in-Florida situation didn't exist, she thought.

She waited for Heather to say something about the Cartier diamond ring, but Heather didn't mention it. Instead she talked about getting together again, soon. She sounded so normal that Liz found herself saying, "I'll call you."

She would, she decided, but she wouldn't go to Heather's place again. Ralph was right when he said any future get-togethers should be in her own apartment where she could control the booze. If drinking had caused Heather's strange behavior, she'd made sure there wasn't so much as a light beer in the fridge.

Before going to sleep that night she thought about the case and reviewed the likely suspects. How things had changed since that first day when she thought Judson might be guilty. Now she was convinced he'd been unjustly accused.

As Ormsby's physician, Dr. Hammond had as much opportunity as Judson to poison him. He too had been left a sizeable sum of money. But why would a doctor with a Park Avenue practice do away with a longtime patient for a quick windfall? If he'd lost all his money through bad investments or gambling, Eichle and Rothman would have found out about it. She crossed the doctor off her list.

Nothing she could think of indicated that Cherie La Salle was the guilty one. Eichle and Rothman must have investigated her thoroughly and they hadn't come up with anything. Scratch Cherie.

That left Clover. Both Sophie and Grandma were convinced she was the guilty one. And Eichle wouldn't have continued to investigate her, even going so far as to fly down to Florida, if he didn't still suspect her. Also, she'd been at the top of her own list from the first. Now Liz came to a definite conclusion. It had to be Clover who'd poisoned Ormsby.

Her heart ached for Judson. She wished there were something she could do to help him. But at least she knew Eichle was trying to dig up evidence that would clear him. Whatever he'd found out, she hoped it was enough to present to Judson's attorney, perhaps even to the D.A.

FOURTEEN

THE NIGHT'S THOUGHTS were still in her mind when she wakened. She wanted to help Judson. But how? If Eichle, in his continuing investigation of Clover, hadn't come up with something, how could she? She was sure Eichle had conferred with Judson's attorney and given him whatever information he'd dug up. Apparently it wasn't enough. Eichle must feel as frustrated as she did, she thought.

Soon after she arrived at her office, Heather phoned. She sounded upset. "Someone from the medical examiner's office just phoned me and asked me to come in," she said. "They have another body. Of course it's not Clover, but the person who phoned said the woman they found has the same measurements as Clover. He said it was a drowning and the facial features wouldn't be recognizable. I don't want to look at her, Liz, but he insisted."

With Eichle officially off the Ormsby case, he wouldn't have been notified, Liz thought. Heather shouldn't have to go through this unpleasant experience alone.

"Do you want me to go with you, Heather?" she asked.

"Oh, Liz—would you?"

"When are you coming in?"

"I'm ready to leave now."

Liz knew Dan would give her permission to meet Heather in the morgue area. "Okay, I'll meet you there," she said.

When she went to Dan's office he was on the telephone. She took up a notepad and wrote on it. *Okay if I meet Heather in the morgue for a possible ID of her sister?* She flashed it at him. He nodded.

Heather arrived at the morgue area soon after Liz got there. Her face showed the strain of her emotions. Liz thought she must be torn between trying to tell herself the body wasn't Clover's and hoping in her heart it was, the ordeal of waiting over.

"Oh, Liz, thank you so much for coming," she said.

Liz patted her shoulder. A few moments later a gurney was wheeled to the window. She saw Heather cringe at the sight of the shrouded body.

When the face was uncovered, Liz could not hold back a gasp. Any recognizable feature had been ravaged. The body must have been washed ashore somewhere, she decided, and fallen prey to scavengers of sea and sky and sand. Heather couldn't possibly identify this woman as Clover.

To her surprise, Heather looked, then nodded. "Yes, that's Clover," she whispered. Just then the door opened and Dan came in. He looked disturbed when he realized Heather had already viewed the corpse.

"I'm terribly sorry," he said. "There's been a mistake. You shouldn't have been called, Miss Prentiss. According to my forensic team this woman is in her mid-forties and has had at least one child."

"She has already identified the body as her sister's," Liz whispered to him.

"I regret this more than I can say, Miss Prentiss," Dan said.

Heather stared through the glass at the gurney being wheeled away. Her voice shook. "I was sure she was Clover. How could I have made such a mistake?"

"You needed closure," Dan replied. Then he suggested that Liz go outside with Heather and make sure she got a taxi.

"He's such a kind man," Heather said, as she and Liz stood outside the building waiting for a cab. Suddenly her tears gushed. "Oh, Liz, I need all the kindness I can get right now. Will you come to my place after work? I don't know if I'll feel up to cooking dinner, but maybe we could order a pizza or something."

Liz remembered her resolve never to go to Heather's place again, but she felt mean and hard-hearted even thinking about saying no. She'd go, she decided, but this time she'd be on her guard.

"I'll come for a little while," she said. "But I can't stay to eat."

Heather smiled and clasped her hand. "Oh, thank you. At least I'll have someone to talk to for a little while."

They hailed a cab. Heather waved as it drove off. Liz went back into the building feeling guilty. She shouldn't have said she couldn't stay for dinner. Heather would have to eat alone—if she ate at all. She might just drink.

It was almost noon when her phone rang. She picked it up, expecting to hear Sophie's voice.

"Rooney?"

It could only be one person. "Yes," she said. "Is that you, Eichle?"

"Right. I need to talk to you. Are you free for lunch?"

"Well…yes…." She was stunned.

"Meet me at Vinny's in fifteen minutes? My treat."

"All right." She couldn't believe this was happening.

"Good. See you there."

What in the world did Eichle want to talk to her about? she wondered, as she walked to the restaurant. The only subject they had in common was Clover. Maybe he'd decided to give her a belated reprimand for being the recipient of Sophie's information out of Homicide.

He was waiting outside the restaurant. "Glad you could make it," he said.

"What's this all about?" she asked.

"I'll tell you when we're settled at a table," he replied.

When they were seated and had ordered, she asked him again, "What's on your mind, Eichle?"

"I was talking to Dennis Dugan this morning," he said.

"You know Dennis?"

"We've been friends since Police Academy."

She had a pretty good idea what they'd talked about—her Saturday-night experience with Heather. She asked him anyway. "So, what did Dennis have to say, and how does it concern *me?*"

"You know Dennis and his wife had been separated for several months and you also know why."

"Yes, that's true."

"Well, he phoned me to tell me they've gotten back together."

"They have? That's great!"

"Dennis told me he owed it all to a suggestion someone made about relocating to a low-crime area, and then he mentioned that person's name. We were surprised we both knew you."

"So I gave him some advice and it worked. You didn't offer to buy me lunch just to tell me that, did you?"

"No. After he told me you were responsible for

saving his marriage, he went on to tell me about your harrowing experience with Heather Saturday night."

She laughed. "Harrowing? That's pretty strong for what happened."

"Don't laugh it off, Rooney. From what Dennis told me, it was a potentially dangerous situation. Locking a door and holding someone against their will is like a kidnapping."

"She'd had too much to drink."

Eichle glowered at her across the table. "I want you to promise me you'll steer clear of Heather from now on."

The intensity of the request startled her. She had no time to give it any thought because the waiter came with their food at that moment. Eichle was the last person she'd ever think would ask her to promise him anything. Dennis must have exaggerated, she decided. "I can't promise you that," she said. "As a matter of fact, I'm going to Heather's place after work today. She had another negative viewing at the morgue this morning. She needs moral support, and I'm the only friend she has."

"You're going to her apartment again? Dennis said you'd agreed you'd only see her at your own place?"

"I know I did, but Heather was terribly upset this morning." She told him what had happened at the morgue.

"Too bad that happened," Eichle said. "I can understand why you want to lend her a little moral support, but…"

"But you still don't want me to go to her apartment."

"Not only that. I want you to avoid her entirely."

He was being unnecessarily harsh, she thought. "Why?" she asked.

"Because she's developing a dependency where you're concerned. I've seen this kind of situation before. If you don't cut this off now she'll be on your tail and in your face every minute. You won't be able to get rid of her."

"You're way off base, Eichle. She has a boyfriend in Florida and she's planning to go back there soon. I think she's tired of trying to convince herself that Clover's alive. That's why she wanted to believe the woman in the morgue this morning was Clover. Dan understood. He said she needed closure."

Eichle frowned. "Sounds like you're determined to go to her place tonight."

"Yes, I am—but only for a little while." She laughed. "Do you think she's going to lock me up again? I told you she'd been drinking when that happened. She never would have done such a thing if she hadn't been smashed."

"She'll have all day to put away plenty of booze," Eichle replied. "And from what you told me about her state of mind, it wouldn't surprise me if she did.

Alcohol triggers something in her. You'd be taking a chance, and this time you might not get out of there as easily as you did before."

"I told her I'd be there and I can't let her down when she's so upset," Liz said.

He was silent for a moment. "Tell you what," he said. "I'll park outside Heather's building while you're in there and if you don't come out in thirty minutes I'll go in and get you."

"Thirty minutes! That's hardly time to say hello."

"You told her you weren't going to stay long, didn't you?"

"Yes, and I appreciate your concern, but Heather won't pull another stunt like that. She was really ashamed of herself when I left Saturday night." As she spoke, Liz recalled that Heather hadn't mentioned the lock-up incident since. It was as if it had never happened. Most likely she was so ashamed of it she'd put it out of her mind.

"There's no negotiating with this," Eichle said. "I want you out of there in thirty minutes, or else."

She knew he wasn't kidding. After all the hostility Eichle had shown her, she had to smile at the concept of him in the role of hero to her rescue.

"Okay, you win," she said. This would be a good time for her to ask him about his continued involvement in the Ormsby case. There was no need to be subtle about it. He knew she'd figured it out when she saw him in Fort Lauderdale. "How's your investigation of the missing twin going?" she asked.

At first he acted cagey. "That investigation is over. I'm on another case now."

"I wasn't talking about an official investigation," she said.

He frowned. "You can't stop meddling in police business, can you?"

"Is it still police business when there's been an indictment and you've been put on another case?"

"It is, until the trial is over."

She gave a sigh of exasperation. "Police business or not, you know I'm involved with Heather and that makes me involved in the case. I didn't deliberately plan it this way but it happened and now I'm just as convinced as you are that Clover poisoned Ormsby. Why can't we talk—compare our ideas? I'll tell you what I've picked up from Heather and you can tell me what you found out in Florida. Maybe, between the two of us, we'll come up with something."

He looked at her with a shake of his head. "No dice."

Her exasperation heightened. "You think I'd be meddling again, don't you? But it's okay for you to meddle in my friendship with Heather."

"That's different," he replied.

She took one last bite of her sandwich, finished her coffee, and got to her feet. "All right," she said,

"I'd better be getting back to the office. Thanks for the lunch."

As she headed for the door he called after her, "Remember, thirty minutes and not one second longer."

FIFTEEN

HEATHER BUZZED HER into the building promptly and met her at the door of her apartment. "I can't thank you enough for coming, Liz," she said. "I've been so upset and confused since this morning. I don't think I could sleep tonight without talking to someone."

"I hope I can help," Liz replied.

They sat down in the living room. "How about coffee?" Heather asked. "I just made some."

Liz nodded. "Thanks, I'd like a cup." This was a welcome switch, she thought. She pictured Eichle sitting outside in his car, imagining a replay of Saturday night. He'd probably be disappointed when it turned out he'd been wasting his time.

She still felt annoyed with him for his curt refusal to discuss what he'd found out about Clover. It must have been something big, yet not big enough to help Judson. But didn't he realize she might know something he didn't? Like a tiny missing piece to a puzzle, it could make everything come together. But he was too stubborn to admit it.

Heather came out of the kitchen with two cups

of coffee. "I remembered you like milk and a little sugar in yours," she said.

"Thanks," Liz said. She watched Heather set the two cups down on the table. Heather's coffee was black. But had she added something other than milk to it while she was in the kitchen? She dismissed the question, telling herself she was thinking like Eichle. "I'm sorry you had to go through that at the morgue this morning," she said. "Someone really messed up."

"It was my mistake too," Heather replied. "I shouldn't have been so quick to say it was Clover, but the body was the same size, even though the face was…" She stopped abruptly and put her head down in her hands.

Liz gave her shoulder a comforting pat. "It was an understandable mistake. The medical examiner explained it perfectly. You wanted to get it over with."

Heather raised her head. "Yes, I did." A look of anguish came to her face. "Oh, Liz, do you think this will ever end?"

Liz wasn't sure what she meant. Did she still think Clover was alive? "I can't answer that," she said, "but there's an old saying—*Time heals all wounds*."

"If she never comes back…if they never find her, I suppose I'll get over this terrible pain, but I'll never stop missing Clover," Heather replied. "Even now it's like I've lost part of me."

"I've never had a sister, so I can't fully imagine

how it would be to lose one—especially an identical twin," Liz said.

Heather finished her coffee and rose from the couch. "I'm ready for a refill. How about you?"

"Not yet," Liz replied. "You go ahead." She watched Heather go to the kitchen. Maybe she should go with her to make sure she didn't add booze, she thought. Again she told herself she was developing an Eichle mentality. Nevertheless, she'd keep alert for telltale sounds—the clink of a bottle, the gurgle of a shot being poured into the cup…

As Heather went into the kitchen, Liz's eyes glanced over the chest near the door. She thought of the photo under the place mats. Again, she felt a sense of something odd about it. But what? It was just a photo of identical twins, wearing shorts and T-shirts, with a background of palm trees. She'd only looked at it twice, and each time the look had been fleeting, yet there was something….

"Did you live in Florida for a long time?" she asked, when Heather came out of the kitchen.

"Oh, no, we moved there only a year ago, after our parents died," Heather replied. "We were living in Topeka, Kansas, at the time."

"It must have been fun, growing up with a twin sister."

"Yes, we had a happy childhood. Our dad's company transferred him to lots of different places in the Midwest, and we always lived in beautiful homes.

But when Clover and I were teenagers we wished we could get out of the Midwest and live someplace glamorous like California or Florida, so when our parents died and we were left alone we moved to Fort Lauderdale."

"Do you have any family out west—aunts and uncles or cousins?"

"Nobody we were close to. We were old enough to be on our own and our parents had left us well-off, and then of course when we got to Florida we went into modeling."

"Will you go back to modeling when you go back to Florida?"

Heather nodded. "I would have signed up with a modeling agency here if Clover hadn't been so depressed. She didn't want to work anymore and I didn't want to leave her alone all day." She sighed. "I kept thinking she'd snap out of it, but that man broke her heart and it will be a long time before she gets over it."

Liz noticed she was still speaking of Clover in the present tense. She decided to change the subject. "What did you think about the Cartier diamond engagement ring being a hoax?" she asked.

"Oh, that," Heather said. "I should have known that man wouldn't order an engagement ring for Clover or any other woman. He was nothing but a playboy with no intentions of marrying."

She didn't seem at all disturbed about discussing

it, Liz thought. This was a switch. The other night the *C and T forever* ring had thrown her out of control. The more she saw of Heather the more she realized how changeable this beautiful young woman was.

"You said your boyfriend is being more reasonable. Does that mean you'll stay in New York awhile longer?" she asked.

"Yes, at least I can give my two weeks notice about moving out of the apartment."

"Are you going to tell Detective Eichle before you leave?"

"Oh, yes. He's been so kind. I wouldn't think of leaving without letting him know."

Heather wouldn't think Eichle was so kind if she knew he was sitting outside in his car, and why, Liz thought. Suddenly she realized her thirty minutes would be up soon and there was something she'd been wanting to ask Heather. She'd been waiting for the right time.

She drew a deep breath. "Heather, did it ever occur to you that Clover might be hiding out somewhere?"

Heather stared at her for a moment. "At first I did think she might have run away," she replied, "but then I decided she just *went* away to be by herself for a while after her heart was broken. Why did you ask me that? Do you think she ran away because she poisoned that man? The police certainly don't think so or they wouldn't have arrested the butler." She shook her head. "Clover couldn't have done such a dreadful thing."

For an instant, Liz thought Heather was on the verge of an angry tirade. Grimacing at the thought of Eichle-to-the-rescue, she hastened to make amends. "I'm sorry if I upset you. I shouldn't have asked you that."

"It's okay," Heather said. "You can ask me anything you want to." Suddenly she smiled. "Are you sure you can't stay and eat with me tonight, Liz?"

"I really can't. I have another commitment." As she spoke, Liz pictured Eichle parked outside the building, checking his watch. She glanced at her own watch, saying, "I should be taking off in a few minutes."

"I remember you told me you'd broken off with your boyfriend," Heather said. "Have you started seeing him again?"

"Oh, no, that's over."

"Are you going out with someone new tonight?"

Liz shook her head. "No—it's nothing like that." It certainly wasn't, she thought, picturing Eichle again.

"I'll be glad to get back with my boyfriend," Heather said.

"Will you let me know when you decide to leave for Florida?" Liz asked.

"Of course I will. You've been a real friend, Liz. I'll never forget you."

"I'll never forget you, either, Heather." *That was no lie!*

"Maybe when you go to visit your parents we can get together."

Liz didn't know how to respond. Visiting Heather in Florida was definitely not on her fun list. "It's quite a drive from Sarasota to Fort Lauderdale," she said.

Heather didn't seem to notice her lack of enthusiasm. "I'm determined to pick up my life where I left off in Florida," she said. "It won't be easy, not knowing…"

Liz knew that Heather would always be haunted by Clover's disappearance. It was surprising that she could talk about it so calmly.

She looked at her watch. "It's time I was going," she said.

"Thanks for coming over," Heather said, as they walked to the door.

She sounded so wistful. Before Liz could hold back the words she heard herself saying, "We'll get together again soon. I'll call you."

Going down on the elevator she told herself she'd like to go to Heather's apartment once more before Heather left for Florida. She wanted to have one last look at the photo in the place-mat drawer. It would be her last chance to figure out why she couldn't keep from thinking about it.

Outside the building she looked down the block

and saw Eichle standing on the sidewalk next to his car. "I was just getting ready to go up and get you," he said, as she approached.

"That would have been totally unnecessary," she replied. "Heather didn't have anything to drink but coffee. She wanted me to stay and eat with her but when I said I couldn't she didn't insist. We had a lovely visit." This was stretching the truth a bit. She hadn't really felt comfortable. But she wasn't going to give him the satisfaction of knowing that.

"I'm glad you enjoyed yourself," he said.

"I would have enjoyed it more if I hadn't known you were parked out here like this was a stakeout," she said.

The instant the words were out she regretted them. He was only trying to make sure she didn't experience another bad scene with Heather. "I'm sorry," she said.

"It's okay," he replied. He opened the car door. "I'll give you a lift home."

"You don't need to do that. The subway's only a short walk."

"I always escort innocent people home after stakeouts," he said.

Could Eichle actually have a sense of humor? she wondered. She got into the car.

"I've been thinking over what you said earlier about us comparing notes on Clover," he said, as he drove the car through the early-evening traffic. "I can't give you any information, but I'd appreciate it if you'd tell me anything you've picked up. It's your duty as a good citizen to come forward with whatever you've found out."

She couldn't believe what she'd heard. He wanted her to tell him everything she knew without giving her any information in return. "I know with your connection to Heather you must have picked up something I haven't," he said. "Here's your chance to put your interest in homicide cases to good use. What do you say, Rooney—is it a deal?"

Some deal, she thought. "I'll think about it," she said.

"I might be going out of town in the next day or so. If I go you'll have plenty of time to think about it," he said.

"I don't suppose you'll tell me where you're going."

"Sure, I will," he replied. "I'm going to Topeka, Kansas—if I go."

She knew why he'd told her. He'd found out that Heather and Clover had last lived in Topeka before Florida. He suspected that Heather had told her this. He was hoping she'd let slip something else Heather had told her—something he might not know. This was a real cat-and-mouse game they were playing.

"How can you leave town in the middle of your new case?" she asked.

"I have some time coming to me and it's an open-

and-shut case—nothing Rothman can't handle for a day or so."

She thought over what he'd said. He *might* be going to Topeka. That meant he'd been trying to get certain information by telephone. If successful, he wouldn't go. She didn't want to let him know she'd figured that out. His hostility towards her had lessened and she wanted to keep it that way. But was his change in attitude a means towards getting her to tell him what she knew about Clover? Had he decided a friendly manner was the best way to get her to open up?

After he dropped her off at her apartment she continued to think about this. There had to be something he hadn't been able to figure out—something he needed to complete his investigation of Clover. Because of her association with Heather, he thought she might have the missing piece to the puzzle.

She couldn't think of anything Heather had told her that Eichle wouldn't have been able to find out. Maybe he'd get this information when he went to Topeka—*if* he went. She remembered Sophie's wild idea, based on the old Bette Davis movie. But Eichle was a shrewd detective. No doubt he'd considered the possibility of one twin assuming the identity of the other. But had he gone so far as to suspect one twin had killed the other? If this had really happened, then the twin she knew as Heather would actually be Clover, and the real Heather would be the missing twin. Also, she'd be dead.

Was this the angle Eichle was working on?

These questions whirled round and round in her mind. By the time she was ready for bed she was in a state of confusion. She couldn't fall asleep. Instead, she kept going over every contact she'd had with Heather, from the first dinner at her own place to this evening's brief visit. She remembered Heather's switch from believing Clover had committed suicide to believing she was alive and suffering from amnesia. She recalled Mrs. Delgado saying she'd seen Clover "yesterday," when Heather had reported her missing the week before.

Then there was the photo. Why hadn't Heather shown it to her? Why was it stashed in a drawer under a pile of place mats?

Should she be a "good citizen" as Eichle had suggested, and tell him about these inconsistencies? Weary from hours of confused thoughts, she grew drowsy. She was almost asleep when a thought flashed out of her subconscious mind. Instantly, she was wide awake. As clearly as if it were there in front of her eyes, she saw the photo of Heather and Clover. Only this time she saw what she'd only half seen in the two fleeting glances. Heather had told her they'd stopped dressing alike when they were rebellious adolescents. *In the Florida photo their shorts and T-shirts were identical. Even their sandals were exactly the same!*

SIXTEEN

THE BURGEONING MORASS of puzzlement and confusion overwhelmed her. She knew she'd had enough of it. She had to tell Eichle about the photo and everything else. Maybe he could unravel the snarl of inconsistencies, and unless he insisted on being the taciturn detective, he'd tell her what it all added up to.

She switched on the light, got the phone book, and looked up his number.

"Eichle—it's Rooney. I hope you weren't asleep."

"*Rooney.* No, I haven't hit the sack yet. What's up?"

"We need to talk."

"Does this mean you've decided to be a good citizen?"

"Call it whatever you want to. What I have to tell you isn't much—it's just some perplexing things I can't figure out. Can we meet for coffee after work tomorrow?"

"Sure."

She heard a note of excitement in his voice. "Don't get your hopes up," she said. "I told you this isn't much."

"It's enough to make you call me in the middle of the night. Maybe you'd better tell me now. I don't want you changing your mind when you wake up tomorrow."

"I promise I won't change my mind."

"Okay, then. The coffee shop near the station, tomorrow after work."

"I'll see you there."

DURING THE MORNING Sophie called her at work. She and Ralph had looked at rings. This took up several minutes before Sophie at last asked, "What's new with you, Liz?"

Liz couldn't resist needling her. "Oh, nothing much, except Eichle gave me a ride home from Heather's last night and I'm meeting him for coffee after work today."

Disbelief sounded in Sophie's voice. "You and *Eichle?*"

Liz laughed. "It's strictly about the Ormsby case. He's agreed to discuss it with me."

"You're going to tell him what you've picked up from Heather?"

"Right."

"Don't forget to tell him about that photo."

"That's at the top of my list. Listen…" She told Sophie about the twin outfits on Heather and Clover. "I think Eichle will be interested in this," she said.

EICHLE TOOK A SWALLOW of his coffee and looked at her across the table. "Well, are you ready to talk?" he asked.

"You make me feel like a witness," she said.

"In a sense, you *are* a witness. You might have important evidence."

"I told you not to expect too much. What I have to tell you isn't going to solve the case."

"Don't be too sure of that," Eichle said. "Often it's the small things that turn out to be important."

"All right." She took a deep breath and began.

He listened without interrupting while she told him about the photo. When she'd finished he made no immediate response. She felt foolish. He'd probably chalked it all up to an overactive imagination. "I told you it wasn't much," she said.

"Not so," he replied. "You're certain Heather said she and Clover refused to dress alike when they were rebellious teenagers?"

"Absolutely."

"And you're sure the photo was taken recently?"

She nodded.

"Two girls in shorts and T-shirts," he said. "Sometimes it's hard to tell the difference between a thirteen-year-old and a twenty-year-old when they're dressed like that. You admitted you didn't get a good look at the picture. Couldn't they have been much younger?"

"No. Heather told me they moved to Florida a year

ago when they were nineteen. That shot was taken in Florida. There were palm trees in the background."

Eichle pondered this for a moment. "And it couldn't have been a photo from an ad they modeled for because they didn't work together."

"Right. What do you make of it, Eichle?"

"I don't know for sure, yet."

"When you're sure, will you let me in on it?"

He laughed. "I'm not sure about *that,* either."

"You're not being fair," she protested. "You said it might be an important piece of evidence."

"I never promised you anything," he replied.

Suddenly she remembered she hadn't told him about Mrs. Delgado's remarks concerning the twins' different personalities or that she'd said she'd seen Clover "yesterday" when Heather had reported her missing the week before. "I left something out," she said.

"Intentionally?"

"No, but now I'm glad I did."

"So you think you have an ace in the hole?"

"Something like that. Promise you'll let me know what you think about the photo and I'll tell you."

"Now who's being unfair? You phoned me at half past eleven last night saying you were willing to talk, and now you're withholding something."

"Oh, it probably isn't worth telling anyway. It's just something Mrs. Delgado said about Clover."

"Who's Mrs. Delgado?"

"The building superintendent's wife. She said something very thought provoking."

"Thought provoking? Now you've got *me* provoked. I could have you served with a subpoena, you know."

She wasn't sure he could if he wasn't officially working on the case. She decided to call his bluff. "So do it," she said.

His keen eyes probed her. It took every ounce of her Irish grit to meet his gaze. "All right," he said. "When I come to a conclusion about the photo, I'll tell you."

"Promise?"

"On my honor as a former Boy Scout and a member of New York's finest."

"Okay. Mrs. Delgado told me Heather was always pleasant and friendly but Clover was unfriendly and barely spoke to her."

"Not surprising," he said. "Good-twin–bad-twin. Go on."

If she'd had any doubts that they were on the same track, that remark would have dispelled them. "There's more," she said. "When I mentioned to Mrs. Delgado that Clover had been away from the apartment since last week, she looked surprised and said she knew she'd seen her the day before."

"Are you suggesting Heather has been hiding Clover in the apartment?"

"No. Heather wouldn't be so broken up if Clover

were still alive. And she wouldn't want me to come to the apartment if she had Clover stashed there. I'm so confused, I don't know what to think. Why would Mrs. Delgado be so sure she'd seen Clover?"

"She could have mistaken Heather for Clover."

"But she said…"

"I know she said Heather was pleasant and friendly and Clover wasn't. But with a few shots of booze under her belt, Heather's personality changes. You know that better than anyone, Rooney."

"Okay, let's say Mrs. Delgado encountered Heather when she'd been drinking and mistook her for Clover. We've cleared that up—but what about the photo?"

"The photo," he said. "I'll have to give that some more thought." He finished his coffee. "This has been a productive talk, Rooney."

"Does that mean what I told you will help?"

"I think there's a chance it might."

"When are you going to Topeka?" she asked.

"I might not have to do. I got some important information by phone today. If I get the rest of it tomorrow morning I'll be able to piece it together with what you told me and figure how it fits."

"Will you call me when you've come to any conclusions?"

"I said I would, didn't I?"

He must be close to figuring it out, she thought. She had to admire him for sticking to his conviction that Judson was innocent. "Does the D.A. know what you've been doing?" she asked.

He laughed. "Your father always said you'd make a good detective. I'll give you a call tomorrow morning if I don't go to Topeka."

SEVENTEEN

LIZ WOKE UP the next morning with a sense of excitement. She was close to getting some answers. Even if Eichle went to Topeka today, he'd let her know his conclusions when he got back.

She'd done the right thing, telling him about the photo and about Mrs. Delgado's comments regarding Clover. She knew he'd figure it all out.

She got to her desk early just in case he called. Every time the phone rang she grabbed it on the first ring. When he hadn't called by noon she decided he'd gone to Topeka. She'd have to wait till he got back to hear how he'd used the information she'd given him, but it would be worth waiting for.

Sophie phoned after lunch. Liz told her what she'd discovered about the photo. "I let Eichle in on it," she said, "and some other things that puzzled me too."

"Twins who never dress like twins, wearing identical outfits in a photo and the photo hidden. I'll bet he thought that was strange. What did he say about that?"

"That interested him more than anything. He said he thinks it could be evidence. He's going to let me know how everything fits into his investigation when he gets back from Topeka."

"Topeka? He didn't go there or anywhere else," Sophie said. "He's been here all day. Are you sure he said he was going out there today?"

Liz felt her high spirits plummet. "He said he'd call this morning if he didn't go."

"Maybe he'll call you later on. You want to meet me after work and fill me in?"

Liz tried to keep her sense of betrayal out of her voice. "Sure. Are you seeing Ralph tonight?"

"Yes, he's meeting me at the six-o'clock ferry and coming home for dinner with the family. Look, I gotta go. See you after work."

Liz hung up the phone. She should have known better than to trust Eichle. He'd taken her information and run with it. He'd never had any intentions of telling her his conclusion. His sudden friendliness was a sham. He still resented what he called "meddling in police matters." This was his way of getting even.

As if this wasn't enough, Heather phoned at three o'clock and told her Eichle had been in touch with her. "He's coming over here this evening," she said. "I think he's going to tell me they're calling off the search for Clover."

Liz was almost too stunned to reply. She knew why Eichle was going to Heather's place. He planned to get a good look at the photo. He knew exactly where it was. Like a fool, she'd told him.

"Are you there, Liz? Did you hear what I said about Detective Eichle coming over?" Heather asked.

"Yes—yes I heard you, Heather. I hope you aren't too upset."

"No, but I wish you could be here with me when he tells me." Her voice broke. "Oh, Liz—could you possibly come over?"

"I'm sorry, I can't make it tonight," Liz replied. She quickly changed the subject. "So I guess you'll phone your boyfriend and tell him it won't be long now."

"Yes, and tomorrow I'll give my notice to Mrs. Delgado."

Heather's voice had calmed at the mention of her boyfriend, Liz thought, after they hung up. But she wouldn't be calm if she knew what Eichle was up to. She pictured him going straight to the chest where she'd told him the photo was stashed, while Heather was in the kitchen making coffee.

Even though he'd double-crossed her, she still had the satisfaction of knowing she'd contributed to his investigation and conclusion. Her information might play a vital role in setting Judson free. Eichle couldn't take that away from her.

"DID EICHLE PHONE YOU?" Sophie asked, when they met after work.

"No, and I'm really ticked off. He promised to phone me if he didn't go to Topeka."

"I heard he was thinking of taking some time off, but why Topeka?"

"That's where Heather and Clover lived before they moved to Florida after their parents died. He probably wants to check records, maybe talk to some schoolteachers—stuff like that."

"He got a call this morning and talked for quite a while," Sophie said. "Maybe it was someone from Topeka. Maybe he got what he wanted and that's why he didn't have to go out there."

"I'm sure that's exactly what happened," Liz said. "He got the information he wanted and hooked it up with what I told him. We had a deal, Sophie, but he just brushed it off. He promised to let me know how his investigation turned out if I gave him whatever information I got from my contact with Heather."

Sophie frowned. "I'm surprised he didn't phone you. Eichle may be a grouch, but he has a reputation for being dependable."

"A man of his word. A straight shooter." Liz's voice crackled with sarcasm. "But you haven't heard the worse of it. Heather told me he's going over to her place tonight. She thinks he's going to tell her they've called off the search for Clover, but I know better. He's planning to take a good look at the photo. That seems to be what he's most interested in. He'll probably scrutinize it while she's making coffee."

"I can't imagine why he'd think the photo would be of any help," Sophie said. "It's just Heather and

Clover dressed alike. So what if they stopped dressing in twin outfits years ago? They could have had
this picture taken just for fun."

"If that's true, why did Heather stash it away?" Liz
asked. "I tell you, there's something strange about
this. I'm sure she has the picture out where she can
see it except when she knows someone's coming over
and then she hides it."

"Do you have any idea what it might have to do
with the case?" Sophie asked.

"Not the slightest. And neither did Eichle when I
told him about it. But I'll bet he knows now, after he
talked to his contact in Topeka." Just thinking about
it stirred her feelings of betrayal all over again.

Her feelings continued to boil after she and Sophie
parted. To try and get her mind off it, she decided
she'd cook herself a special dinner. She stopped at a
market on her way home and bought fresh shrimp and
all the other fixings for a dish Mom used to make,
shrimp creole. She knew it would take a lot of time
and effort to prepare, but she hoped she could work
off some of her anger and resentment.

She made sure she bought enough shrimp so she'd
have plenty left over. She'd freeze what she didn't eat
right away. Her feelings wouldn't disappear overnight, but at least she'd have a few gourmet dinners
to comfort her.

While she prepared the shrimp she couldn't keep
from thinking about Eichle going over to Heather's

place. He was probably there right now. She hoped Heather would catch him red-handed, rummaging through the place-mat drawer.

About an hour later the shrimp creole was almost ready. She was tossing a green salad when her door-bell rang. When she looked through the peephole she felt her anger flare anew. The face on the other side of the door was Eichle's. She threw open the door and confronted him. "You have some nerve showing up here after you ran out on our deal," she snapped.

"Before your redheaded temper gets out of control, will you let me in so I can explain?" he asked.

She stepped aside and waved him in. "This better be good," she said.

From behind the kitchen screen came the mouth-watering aroma of shrimp creole.

Eichle sniffed the air, saying, "Whatever you're cooking, it smells great."

That sounded like a hint, she thought. But surely he wouldn't expect a dinner invitation after his double-cross. "Never mind what I'm cooking. Just tell me why you ditched our deal," she said.

"Do you think I'd be here if I intended to go back on my word?" he asked. "If you'll simmer down and listen…"

"All right," she said. They sat down on the couch.

"I know I said I'd call you this morning, but it

wasn't till this afternoon that I had anything to work with," he said.

"Then why didn't you call me this afternoon?"

"I wanted to wait till I put it all together."

"Does that include the results of your visit to Heather's apartment this evening?"

"It does. I left there a couple of hours ago. Since then I've been working hard on this. How did you know I was going over there?"

"She phoned me and told me. She thought you were going to tell her the search for Clover is being called off."

"I did. But it wasn't just an excuse to go over there. It will be off the end of the week."

"And after you told her I suppose she offered you coffee and while she was in the kitchen you looked for the photo."

"Right. It was in the drawer where you said it would be."

By this time her anger had receded. "Did you have time to get a good look at it?"

"Better than that." With a grin, he reached into his coat pocket.

Liz gasped when he brought out the photo. "How could you do something so risky? When she goes to look for it she'll know you took it."

"Don't worry about it," he said. "Just listen to this. I took a good, long look at it when I got out to the car. This photo was spliced with a duplicate photo.

It's not a shot of Heather and Clover—it's the same twin twice. Here, see for yourself."

Liz examined the photo. On close scrutiny she saw not only two identical young women wearing identical clothing but also identical palm trees, even to the same curled frond on each one. A faint line of demarcation was also visible. For a moment she was too stunned to speak. "Is this Heather?" she managed to ask.

He nodded. "It is."

"But why did she have the photo made like this?"

"To support her delusion that she and Clover were in Florida together."

"I don't understand. Clover *was* in Florida with her."

He shook his head. "Clover died over a year ago in Kansas, in the same accident as their parents. The trauma of suddenly losing her twin and her parents too was more than Heather could take."

The startling words settled into Liz's mind. Pieces of the puzzle began to fit together. All this time Heather had been living in a delusional world—a world where Clover was still alive. The photo was part of the delusion. For a few moments she was too shocked to speak or to think beyond this revelation.

Eichle's voice came into her bewilderment. "She should have had psychiatric help after the accident. Instead, she moved to Florida, imagining Clover was with her."

Still dazed, Liz could only think of Heather's mental state. "Psychiatry could help her now, couldn't it?" she asked. "It's not too late, is it?"

"In a way it's too late," Eichle replied.

She stared at him in puzzlement before the truth hit her like a bolt of lightning. It was too late for Theodore Van Brunt Ormsby. It was Heather who'd poisoned him!

EIGHTEEN

"ARE YOU OKAY, ROONEY?"

"Sure, except for feeling as if I'd been kicked in the stomach."

"Did you develop a real friendship with Heather?"

"It was more pity than anything else. She seemed so pathetic. I wanted to help her. It's a shock finding out she's capable of killing someone."

"She had me fooled for a while too," Eichle said.

"But you must have suspected something when you told me to steer clear of her."

"I got a hunch something wasn't right when she locked you in her apartment. Like I told you, I thought she was developing a dependency on you. That plus her drinking spelled trouble. But I was still a long way from suspecting she'd poisoned Ormsby. I was still concentrating on Clover."

With the initial shock wearing off, Liz's mind filled with questions. "When are you going to the D.A. with this?"

"I've already been there. I phoned him after I left Heather's place. But first I stopped at the precinct and made a copy of the photo. I had no backup for my information from Topeka. Clover's death certificate won't be faxed till tomorrow. And I had no verification that Heather locked you in her apartment. I wasn't sure he'd take immediate action without some tangible evidence of her instability."

"Why did it take so long to find out Clover died in the accident? All you had to do was check the Bureau of Vital Statistics, or whatever they call it in Topeka."

"Heather neglected to tell us she changed her name when she moved to Florida. Her family name is really Prenzik, so when I started my investigation of the twins' background, I got nowhere with Prentiss."

"I guess she thought Prentiss would be a classier name for a model," Liz said. "You must have had to dig for her real name. How did you do it?"

"I went after birth records of twin girls born twenty years ago in all the places Heather told us they'd lived before they moved to Topeka. Once I found twin girls named Heather and Clover Prenzik, I had a name to go on, and the rest was easy."

"Will the charges against Judson be dropped?"

"The wheels are already in motion. The D.A.'s meeting with Judson's attorney this evening. By the way—the D.A. will need your statement about Heather locking you in her apartment. You'll probably get a call from his office tomorrow."

"What's going to happen to Heather?"

"She'll be taken into custody, probably sometime

tonight. Under the circumstances, she'll be admitted to a hospital for psychiatric evaluation."

At that moment Liz's cooking timer sounded. The shrimp creole was done and she was hungry. She felt an easing of her shock and tension. "Do you like shrimp creole, Eichle?" she asked.

"Who doesn't? Is this a dinner invitation?"

"Yes. Can you stay?"

"You're asking someone who hasn't had a real home-cooked meal since last Christmas if he'd like to stay for shrimp creole?"

She laughed. "I'll take that as a yes."

"Anything I can do to help?" he asked, as she went behind the screen.

"Yes. You can open up the gateleg table."

"Gateleg table?" His voice sounded puzzled.

"It's next to the couch." He definitely wasn't into interior decorating, she thought.

"Okay, I have it." A moment later she heard sounds of table legs being swung out and leaves put in place. "Done," he said. "Anything else?"

She stepped from behind the screen and got place mats, paper napkins, and cutlery out of a chest drawer. "You can set the table if you want to. Everything's ready."

When they sat down to eat, he took his first forkful and gave a groan of satisfaction. "This tastes great. Do you eat like this all the time?"

"No. You just happened to drop by when I was

furious with you and about to placate myself with a gourmet dinner."

"I hope you're already placated."

"Yes, I am. You did a good job of explaining."

"We haven't touched on everything. If you have any more questions, fire away."

"Okay. Did you pick up any clues in Fort Lauderdale?"

"Nothing much. I sensed something when the woman at the modeling agency told me Heather and Clover never worked as twins, but she didn't seem to think anything of it. She said they wanted to make it as individuals."

"Like not wearing twin outfits. Anything else?"

"I got their condo address from the agency and questioned some neighbors there. I was told they kept to themselves. Nobody saw much of them. One neighbor remarked she'd heard they were identical twins but she'd never seen the two of them together."

"You'd think someone would have figured out there was only one of them."

"Someone would have picked up on it eventually."

"Heather lived there for a year. It's amazing that in all that time nobody got wise."

Eichle gave a wry smile. "Remember, I didn't get wise right away, myself. Heather was very clever. She told people she and her twin sister were living in the condo together. She got into modeling work as

Heather and then as Clover. Since they didn't work together on shoots, nobody at the modeling agency ever saw them together, either. Nobody realized there was no Clover."

Heather had pulled the same stunt when she rented her New York apartment, Liz thought. Mrs. Delgado hadn't the slightest inkling that her twin tenants were one and the same. It never occurred to her that she'd never seen them together. She recalled what Mrs. Delgado had said about the difference in the twins' personalities. Eichle had reminded her that Heather's personality changed when she'd been drinking. Now she asked herself if this could be kind of a Jekyll-and-Hyde thing. Was it possible that Heather's mind sometimes led her to believe she was Clover?

"I know this sounds silly, but do you think there might be times when Heather sort of *becomes* Clover?" she asked.

"It's not silly. In her sadly mixed-up mind it's quite possible, especially when she's had a few drinks. A shrink might say she has multiple personality disorder."

"Then she won't serve a prison sentence, will she? She'll be put in some kind of mental hospital."

A slight frown crossed his face. "Something keeps bugging me about all this. Heather might have deluded herself into believing Clover was still alive and living with her in Florida, but when she had that photo spliced she must have known Clover was dead."

Liz thought about this for a moment. He was right, she decided. Heather wanted a picture of herself with Clover in Florida. She knew this wasn't possible, so she faked it with two shots of herself. She remembered telling people they hadn't dressed alike for years. Maybe she thought she'd told Eichle too. She knew exactly what she was doing. That's why she hid the photo every time she expected visitors.

"Is it possible she goes back and forth between sanity and insanity?" she asked.

He laughed. "That's for the shrinks to determine. It could be that she's just very clever. The way she came into the station and reported her twin sister missing and then not giving us her real name—it makes me wonder."

"Are you suggesting that poisoning Ormsby and reporting her twin sister missing was a clever plan to get away with murder?"

"I ask myself that question every time I think of the photo. There's no doubt she's mentally disturbed, but to what degree? The D.A. said the photo will play a big part in deciding whether or not she's sane enough to stand trial."

"How did the D.A. react when you told him you'd been conducting your own investigation?"

"He didn't blow up. He knew he'd made a mistake arresting Judson, and now he can admit it without looking bad. Once the news media latches on to Heather the public will forget about Judson."

"Not me," she replied.

"That's because you've met the man. You've talked with him…." He grinned. "I'll never forget him offering you coffee and you sitting yourself down at the kitchen table."

"I know you weren't pleased about that."

"No, but I would have been even less pleased if I'd known you were going to interview the security guard before I even got to the lobby. You knew about the female visitor before I did."

"Is this where I'm supposed to say I'm sorry for meddling in police business?"

"You know you had too good a time with this case to be sorry."

"You got that right. It's the most interesting case I've ever followed." She studied his face for some sign of his former hostility. She saw none. But that didn't mean he didn't still harbor those feelings. "Do you still resent me?" she asked.

He smiled. "How could I, when you helped me solve this case?"

He couldn't very well say he resented her while finishing the best meal he'd had since Christmas, she thought. This was probably just a temporary truce. Suddenly she recalled how angry he'd been in Fort Lauderdale when he found out she was getting information about the case from Sophie, yet he hadn't done anything to make trouble for her or for Sophie. Now would be a good time to ask him about that.

"Why didn't you report Sophie Pulaski for passing homicide information on to me?" she asked. "And why didn't you try and have me barred from any more murder scenes or morgue viewings?"

He took a forkful of shrimp creole before answering. "Sophie has the makings of a good cop. I didn't want to interfere with her chances. And as for you…" His cell phone sounded at that moment. After a brief, monosyllabic exchange, he turned it off. "I must go," he said. "Heather's been taken into custody tonight." He glanced at his dinner plate upon which only one small morsel of shrimp creole remained. "I would have asked for seconds," he said. "Thanks for feeding me, Rooney."

What a difference an hour or so could make, she thought, as she cleared the table. Her spirits were right back where they were when she woke up this morning. In fact, she felt even more elated. This was the first case where she'd have legal participation. Eichle said the D.A. considered the photo important evidence and he'd need her statement. She'd probably get a call from his office tomorrow.

She thought of Judson. By now he'd been notified that the charges against him were being dropped. This was also the first case where she'd helped free an erroneously indicted suspect.

While she washed the dishes she thought of

Heather. She reviewed their association from their first talk in the coffee shop. She recalled the sadness in Heather's eyes that evening and the subsequent evenings of tearful reminiscing about Clover and how close they were and how she thought Clover must have amnesia. How much of this was genuine and how much a cover-up for a vengeful murder?

Later, she tried to lose herself in a best-seller, but her thoughts kept returning to Heather. She thought about the drinking. Was this Heather's way of seeking solace for her grief, or was it an escape from her dark secret?

She thought of Heather being arrested. When the knock sounded on her door and she heard the loud call, "Police. Open up!" would she know why they'd come? When they read her her rights, would she understand? When they handcuffed her, would her tears and confusion be real, or would she be pretending?

Eichle had said it was up to psychiatrists to determine her level of sanity. The thought of Eichle reminded her of his hasty departure. The arrest could be taking place at this very moment. Maybe there'd be something about it on TV.

She put down her book, switched on the TV, and turned to the news channel. For several minutes she watched clips of a golf tournament and then an interview with one of the principals in the latest Hollywood scandal. It was too early for anything about it to be on, she thought, though Eichle had bolted out of here as if it were going to happen early this evening. Even if it had, it would take time for the word to get out to the news media, she decided. It could be midnight before there'd be anything on TV.

She was about to turn off the set when the Hollywood interview was suddenly blanked by an announcement. *"We interrupt this program to bring you a late-breaking news bulletin."*

The news flash was brief. It stated only that new evidence in the Theodore Van Brunt Ormsby murder had resulted in the release of indicted suspect Charles Judson and the arrest of Heather Prentiss, the woman who reported her sister missing the day after the murder. *"We now return to the program in progress,"* the announcer said. *"Stay tuned for film coverage of the arrest."* Nothing was said about the sisters being twins. Liz knew that would come later, when the news media got all the details.

She didn't have to stay tuned long before shots of the arrest came on showing Heather being taken out of her apartment in handcuffs. Though the camera zoomed in on her, Liz caught a glimpse of Eichle and Rothman as they escorted her to the waiting squad car. Heather looked strangely calm as she was led through the crowd of reporters and curious onlookers. She stared straight ahead as if she didn't even see them. But just as she got to the car someone called out, "Why did you do it?" She turned around. With the camera focusing on her face and tears brimming her eyes, she said, "You don't understand. It was Clover."

NINETEEN

THE NEXT MORNING Heather's arrest was all over early-morning TV. While eating breakfast, Liz watched reruns of last night's news and listened to updates.

The name of the hospital where Heather had been taken was not disclosed. This was to avoid a frenzy of reporters and photographers at the facility, Liz decided. She wondered how long it would take for the press to find out.

The Delgados were interviewed. Mr. Delgado said the twins in apartment 2-A were very nice ladies and good tenants who never bothered him. It was clear he hadn't quite gotten it yet that there were never two ladies in Apartment 2-A.

Mrs. Delgado claimed she knew there was something fishy about the twins from the first. "One of them was nice and friendly and the other wouldn't hardly speak to me," she said. "So, now you say it was the same one all the time, but I'm telling you it was like there was two different girls up there." She also mentioned she lived in the apartment below 2-A and she heard very few sounds from the apartment above. "With two girls you'd think there'd be more walking around and talking and more bathroom noise. When I asked my husband didn't he think that was strange, he said we should be glad we had two nice, quiet tenants."

Also interviewed was the security guard at Ormsby's condo tower. He said he knew all along Heather was the one he'd seen go up to the penthouse.

On her way to work Liz passed a newsstand and glanced at the first page of the *New York Times*. Quiet headlines and a brief article revealed the latest development: New Arrest In Ormsby Poisoning—D.A. Drops Charges Against Judson. She didn't buy a copy. Dan always had one in the office. Besides, there'd be more coverage in the tabloids later. She wasn't ashamed to admit she enjoyed the offbeat headlines and the photos.

Soon after she got to her desk, Sophie phoned, all excited about Heather's arrest. "I didn't hear about it till late last night. The first thing I thought of was that Eichle had used the information you gave him to convince the D.A. Is that what happened?"

"Not exactly," Liz replied. "I'll tell you all about it when I see you.'

"Let's have dinner somewhere tonight. Ralph's on duty."

Liz remembered she had shrimp creole left over. Even though Eichle had ploughed into it as if it were his first square meal in weeks, there was enough for two more meals. "How about meeting at my place?

Last night I made a shrimp dish from one of my mother's recipes and even after Eichle filled up on it there's plenty left for us."

"*Eichle?* You had Eichle over for dinner last night?"

Liz laughed. "I'll fill you in on it tonight. See you later."

A few minutes after they'd hung up, the D.A.'s office called, asking her to come in this morning and give a statement relative to the Ormsby case. She went to tell Dan. Since he was unaware of how far she had gone into the case, she had to give him a complete rundown.

He listened and broke into a broad smile. "Not only did you provide evidence, but you're a witness," he said. "This will tickle your father."

"I wouldn't have missed this for anything. And I owe it all to you, Dan, not only for letting me go along to Ormsby's penthouse with you, but for taking me to the morgue that day. Seeing Heather there was the start of it all." She sighed. "There'll never be another case like this. From now on they'll all seem tame."

"I hope you'll consider all the homicides during the next couple of weeks too tame to bother with," he said. "I'm going on vacation next week."

She knew what he meant. With another doctor covering for Dan, she wouldn't enjoy the privileges she got from him. "Don't stay away too long," she told him, with a smile.

After lunch she gave her statement at the D.A.'s office. An aide took it. The Big Man himself was probably too ashamed of his Judson blunder to come face-to-face with her, she thought.

On her way home after work she bought the *Daily News*. Just as she expected, the latest development in Ormsby's murder was featured on the front page with a photo of Heather and blaring headlines. Model Arrested In Playboy Poisoning. The photo showed Heather wearing a bikini. The newspaper must have gotten it from the modeling agency in Fort Lauderdale, Liz decided. That wasn't all they got. Statements from startled people at the agency and neighbors in the condo appeared in articles on the two inside pages.

Photos of Heather being taken into custody also appeared, with an article about her belief that her dead twin sister was still alive. A full description of the circumstances was given. Freak Fantasy Prompted Poisoning the headline proclaimed.

A photo of Heather's boyfriend and an interview with him covered two columns. The headline read Batty Beauty's Boyfriend Baffled. Liz read it through. He was quoted as saying Heather would never have moved to New York if her twin sister hadn't insisted on it. Like Mr. Delgado, the bizarre situation hadn't hit home. Not surprising, Liz thought. She hadn't quite gotten used to it herself.

She'd just walked in the door of her apartment when Mom and Pop phoned. Of course they'd heard the news about Heather. When Liz told them the part she'd played in Heather's arrest and Judson's release, Pop laughed and said again she'd make a good detective. Mom expressed concern about her involvement with a crazy woman. Lucky she didn't know about that Saturday night episode, Liz thought.

Sophie arrived, bursting with questions. Liz wasn't sure which she was more curious about, Heather's arrest or the idea of Eichle being invited to dinner. "Did he talk his way out of the double-cross?" she asked. "I guess he must have phoned and explained, but why in the world did you ask him to have dinner with you?"

"He didn't phone. He dropped by while I was cooking the shrimp creole and after he explained…" She stopped abruptly. "Aren't you going to ask me about Heather?"

"Oh, sure, but I couldn't help wondering why you'd invited a grouch like Eichle to eat with you. So how about Heather? Talk in Homicide is she might be judged not fit to stand trial. Does she really think Clover's alive and been living with her all this time? Did you hear what she said on TV last night?"

Liz nodded. She could still see Heather's beautiful, tearful face and hear her words, "You don't understand. It was Clover."

"It certainly seems as if she believes Clover is alive, but Eichle thinks there are times when she knows exactly what's going on." She told Sophie about the photo being spliced.

Sophie stared at her in surprise. "She faked the photo? She has to be off her rocker to do something like that." She thought about it for a moment. "But she must have known when she had it spliced that Clover had died. I think she knew what she was doing."

"Eichle thinks so, and I do too."

"Do you think Clover—I mean Heather—meant to kill Ormsby when she put Judson's medicine in his coffee?"

"I don't know. Maybe she didn't have murder on her mind when she went to the penthouse, but after he told her he had no intentions of marrying her she might have gone into a homicidal rage."

"What would she have done if Judson's medicine wasn't on the table?"

"Picked up a kitchen knife, maybe."

Sophie shuddered. "Do you really think she'd get that violent?"

Liz recalled the strange smile on Heather's face the night she'd locked the door. She hadn't been too far away from violence then. "Maybe Eichle's right about the split personality," she said. "Maybe one side of her is capable of stabbing someone."

"I get the creeps every time I think of you being in her apartment," Sophie said.

"I know I was lucky—but if I hadn't ever gone there I wouldn't have discovered the photo. The D.A. says it's important evidence. Oh—I forgot to tell you, I gave my statement today and I'll be called to testify if there's a trial."

"Good. And the photo will show she's not off in la-la land all the time."

Liz nodded. "It's like her mind was okay when she got the picture spliced, but then the photo became part of her delusion.'

"It's so weird," Sophie said.

Liz turned on the TV. "Let's watch the news while we eat. Maybe there'll be something new on about the case."

An interview with Judson was in progress. *"How does it feel to be a free man, Mr. Judson?"* Stupid question, Liz thought. Evidently Judson thought so too. He just smiled, and shook his head. *"What are you planning to do with the money Mr. Ormsby left you?"* This time Judson answered the question. With true British dignity he said he'd prefer to keep this to himself. The interview ended on that note.

Sophie laughed. "He should have said, 'Butt out, it's none of your business.'"

Next, a prominent psychiatrist was introduced. "Thanks for agreeing to this interview, Doctor," the commentator said. "Could you give us your opinion of Heather Prentiss's mental state?"

The psychiatrist, a bearded man perhaps in his early sixties, responded. "While I am not among the physicians conducting the psychiatric evaluation of Miss Prentiss, I have treated a number of patients whose symptoms seem to correspond with hers. I base my opinion upon my observations of Miss Prentiss when I saw her on television last night, and what I read in the newspaper this morning."

"This will be interesting," Sophie said. "I know whatever the psychiatrists examining Heather decide, they won't talk about it before the hearing. But this guy might give us some idea."

The doctor continued. "I believe Miss Prentiss could be suffering from a mental aberration known as Dissociative Disorder."

"Could you explain what that is?"

"It's a disruption of the usually integrated functions of consciousness, memory, and identity."

Liz looked at Sophie. "I'm not sure what he said, but the part about memory and identity sounds like he's on the right track."

"This disruption may be gradual, transient, or chronic," the doctor went on. "It may involve delusion, depression, dissociative amnesia, and aggressive impulses."

"Wow," Sophie said. "That's Heather all right."

"It certainly is," Liz replied. "It puzzled me when

she'd talk incessantly about her boyfriend and going back to Florida but then the next time I saw her she wouldn't even mention him. I guess that would come under the amnesia part of it."

"And how about aggressive impulses. That sounds like a polite name for violent behavior," Sophie said. "This guy knows what he's talking about."

Just then the psychiatrist was asked if he believed Heather was fit to stand trial. He declined to answer directly. "Without having examined Miss Prentiss I don't feel qualified to make that judgment," he replied. "As I said, I came to my conclusions by observing her conduct on television and reading about her past history in the newspapers." The interview ended. A commercial came on. Liz turned off the TV. "Let's forget Heather for a while and enjoy our dinner," she said.

"Okay by me. This shrimp thing is really good."

"It's one of Mom's recipes."

"I know Ralph would go for it. Will you tell me how to make it so I can practice cooking it before we get married?"

"Sure. Remind me to write it down for you before you leave. It's a dish men seem to like. I know it's a favorite with Pop and my brother." And it had made a big hit with Eichle too, she thought. Suddenly she remembered he'd dashed off last night without answering her question. Why hadn't he made trouble for her after he found out she was getting information from Sophie? She'd probably never get a chance to ask him again. She might run into him at some future murder scene, but with this investigation over, he didn't need her input anymore. Most likely the next time she saw him he'd have gone back to his old, disapproving attitude. Too bad, she thought. For a while it was almost as if they could have been friends.

TWENTY

THE NEXT DAY, a reaction set in. The Ormsby poisoning had taken over her thoughts every day for the past three weeks, from her first waking moments till her last before she slept. Now her involvement in it was gone. Without it she felt a sense of emptiness. "I feel like a kid who's lost a favorite toy," she told Sophie on the phone the following Monday.

"Cheer up," Sophie said. "There's sure to be another murder soon, and it might be even more interesting than the playboy poisoning. Maybe some obnoxious celebrity will be next."

"If something like that happens, I hope it's not during the next couple of weeks. Dan's on vacation. I couldn't go to the murder scene or get in on autopsy reports or anything."

"Do you know who's covering for Dan?"

"A Dr. Tyrone Jackson. I've never met him, but even if he's easy to get along with I can't waltz into his office and say I expect him to take me along to the next murder scene."

"Heather's psychiatric tests should be ready for

the hearing pretty soon," Sophie said. "And you'll be called to testify. That will liven things up for you."

Liz sighed. "Poor Heather. I wonder how she's doing, wherever she is."

"Well, at least we know she's not in a jail cell. I'm surprised the news media hasn't found out where they took her."

"I hope they never do. There'd be photographers posted outside the hospital twenty-four hours a day, waiting for a glimpse of her at a window."

"They might even get camera people and reporters inside the hospital disguised as nurses and orderlies," Sophie said.

Liz laughed. "I think that only happens in movies."

"It's getting busy around here. I gotta go," Sophie said. "I'll call you later."

Still thinking about Heather, Liz hung up the phone. Eichle must know where she'd been taken, she thought. He could have at least let her know if Heather was comfortable and being treated well. Maybe he thought she didn't care.

Besides hoping some super-inquisitive news reporter didn't ferret out where Heather was, she hoped the case would not go to court. A billionaire playboy, a beautiful woman spurned, a murder of vengeance. It had all the elements to develop into a circus. This would only confuse and disturb Heather further. Though she agreed with Eichle that Heather had her moments of sanity, those moments might disappear forever if she were subjected to a news-media frenzy.

WHEN HER PHONE RANG in the midafternoon she expected to hear Sophie's voice. Instead, she heard the familiar "Rooney?"

"Hello, Eichle." Was he calling to let her know how Heather was? Maybe he wasn't as much of a grouch as she'd thought.

"Judson wants to take us out for dinner tonight," he said. "Can you make it?"

She was too surprised to answer immediately. This was Judson's way of saying thanks. He knew Eichle had been instrumental in getting the indictment overturned. His attorney must have told him about her part in it.

"I know it's short notice. I should have phoned you earlier," Eichle said.

"You knew about this earlier?"

"Yes, since this morning, but I've been tied up. So, what do you say, is it yes or no?"

What would the three of them talk about during dinner? she wondered. The one topic they had in common was the case. What if Judson seemed reluctant to discuss it? What if Eichle were the one who didn't want to talk about it? She pictured them dining in total silence. However, it could go the other way. Judson might want to know how Heather's tests were proceeding and when the hearing might take place. Eichle might loosen up and at least tell them something.

"Yes, I can make it," she said. "Where and what time?"

"The Plaza at seven. Judson said he'd made reservations."

"Okay, I'll meet you at the Plaza a few minutes before seven."

She smiled as she hung up the phone. Judson was already making good use of his legacy. She doubted if he'd ever reserved a table at the Plaza in his own name while Ormsby was alive.

SOPHIE PHONED just before quitting time. "Can you make it for coffee before I meet Ralph?"

"Sure," Liz replied. She knew their meetings for coffee after work were numbered. Soon, Sophie would be caught up in wedding plans. And after she and Ralph were married she'd want to hurry home to their apartment after work.

Sophie's marriage would mark the end of an era, she thought, as she hung up the phone. A part of life she'd known for almost twenty years was already being phased out. She knew she'd miss it.

While waiting for Sophie at the newsstand she bought a tabloid. The headlines and front-page photo were about a ruckus between a prominent city politician and his socialite wife in a Manhattan supper club. The photo showed the wife dousing her husband over the head with the contents of her wineglass.

The Ormsby case had been relegated to two articles on page three. Liz scanned the headlines. Psycho Twin May Not Stand Trial For Playboy Poisoning. Nothing new there, she thought. She went to the other article. Boyfriend Blasts Borgia. She'd wondered how long it would be before some tabloid reporter would compare Heather to the notorious Lucretia. In the interview, the Florida boyfriend was quoted as saying he now realized Heather had been lying to him all along. She'd told him she had the flu for a week, when she was really seeing that billionaire. She'd made a fool of him and he was through with her.

Was Heather allowed to read newspapers in the hospital? Liz wondered. If she saw this article it would be a mercy if she happened to have her recurring amnesia.

WHEN LIZ AND SOPHIE settled themselves in the coffeehouse, Sophie said, "How about having dinner with Ralph and me tonight?"

Sophie must have sensed she felt a little blue, Liz thought. That's the way it had always been between them. "Thanks," she said. "Any other night I'd jump at the chance, but…" She decided to tease Sophie. "I'm dining at the Plaza with two gentlemen."

She laughed at the astounded look on Sophie's

face. "If you're surprised now, wait till I tell you who the gentlemen are—Eichle and Judson."

"Oh," Sophie said. "I was hoping you'd started seeing a new guy and he wanted you to meet his father. How in the world did this happen?"

"Judson's treating us to dinner. I guess he wants to thank us."

"Maybe you'll talk about the case and Eichle will tell you how Heather is."

"I hope so, but I'm not counting on it."

"I know you're feeling low tonight and I understand," Sophie said. "You've been on a high since this case broke, and now you've come down. But it's not over as far as you're concerned. Even if Eichle doesn't keep you informed, don't forget you're going to testify at the hearing. That makes you still very much involved."

She knew Sophie was still trying to bolster her spirits. "With your upbeat reminders I feel a lot better," she said.

After their coffee, Liz went home to change into something appropriate for dinner at the Plaza. The tan pants, dark blue blazer, and white shirt she'd had on all day would have passed, but as long as she had the time, she might as well put on the green suit she'd bought while she was dating Wade. She remembered she'd paid too much for it. She'd been trying to impress him and it had worked. He'd told her it brought out the green in her eyes. It had certainly brought out the green from her wallet, she thought with a rueful smile. Well, maybe it would impress Eichle and he'd let her know what was going on with Heather.

She took a cab to the Plaza and got there at quarter of seven. When she entered the lobby, Eichle was already there. "Judson's coming from Brooklyn. He probably won't be along for a few minutes," Eichle said. "We could have a drink in the bar while we're waiting or, if you'd rather, we could just sit here in the lobby."

"Let's sit here and talk," she replied. "Am I allowed to ask about Heather?"

He nodded. "Sure, but I don't have all the answers. The doctors aren't making any statements."

"I don't expect a psychiatric report. I only want to know if she's comfortable where she is. Can you tell me before Judson gets here? He might not want to talk about the case, especially about Heather."

"Not so. When Judson phoned me this morning he asked about Heather. I'll tell you exactly what I told him. I haven't seen her since the night of the arrest because I can't risk being tailed by reporters. But she's in an excellent facility and, according to the D.A., one of the best defense attorneys in the city is taking her case."

"There hasn't been anything in the news about an attorney," Liz said. "Is this being kept quiet?"

"Yes. For as long as possible. He's somewhat of a legal celebrity. When the newshounds get wind of him making visits to the hospital, they'll figure out that's where Heather is."

"How did she manage to hook up with this hotshot attorney?"

"Through one of the psychiatrists at the hospital."

"The psychiatrist must think she deserves a good defense. Maybe this means the doctors believe she shouldn't be held responsible for what she did."

"I've seen more than one homicidal maniac get off because of psychiatric testimony and a clever lawyer," Eichle said.

"Homicidal maniac! Is that what you think Heather is?"

He laughed. "Okay—so the term was too strong. But whether or not Heather is judged fit for trial, she needs to be confined to a mental hospital."

"I agree. Maybe, with treatment and medication, her mind can be healed."

"I've seen that happen too," Eichle replied.

He'd been watching the entrance while they talked. "Here comes Judson," he said.

The ordeal of his arrest had taken its toll on Judson, Liz thought. He appeared to have lost weight. His face was drawn. "Good evening," he said, with a slight bow. "I'm pleased you could join me."

"We're pleased too," Liz said. "It's good to see you again, Judson."

"Thanks for asking us," Eichle said.

"It was the least I could do for the two of you," he replied. "Shall we see if our table is ready?"

When they were seated and had ordered, Liz was surprised when he immediately inquired about Heather. "Do you know when Miss Prentiss's hearing is to be scheduled?" he asked.

"The D.A. can't move on that till her psychiatric tests are completed," Eichle replied.

Liz wondered how Judson felt about the hearing. Did he, like Eichle, think Heather should be judged fit to stand trial?

"Meanwhile, I'm still going over possible evidence," Eichle continued. "Today I reviewed some articles collected at the scene."

Wouldn't the spliced photo show that Heather was sane enough to be tried? Liz asked herself.

As if he'd guessed her thoughts, Eichle added, "The D.A. is confident we have what we need, but I wanted to make sure we haven't overlooked anything."

"So you took another look at the evidence kits," Liz said. "Did you come up with anything new?"

"And if you did, are you at liberty to discuss them?" Judson asked.

Eichle nodded. "It's just something I'm curious about. I was planning to question you about this, Judson. I might as well do it now." He glanced at Liz. "It's okay for you to be in on this, Rooney. You know when to keep your mouth shut."

She knew he meant this as a compliment. Coming from him, it ranked right up there with "You look gorgeous."

"There was a small leather jewelry box in one of the kits," he said. "I'd like to know how it figures in the case. It was found on the kitchen table. Did you happen to notice it that morning when you came back from your day off, Judson?"

Judson shook his head. "No. It must have been behind a bowl of fruit. But I know it wasn't there the previous morning before I left. I would have seen it because I placed the fruit bowl on the table myself."

Eichle paused to jot this information in his notebook. Liz took advantage of the pause. "What was in the box?" she asked.

"A pearl-and-gold pendant," he replied. "Ormsby must have put it on the table himself. The only clear prints on the box were his."

"How could that be?" Liz asked. "Wouldn't it have gotten clerks' and customers' fingerprints on it in the jewelry shop?"

"Evidently the leather was buffed before it left the shop and it was handled carefully to avoid smudging," Eichle said. He turned to Judson. "Do you have any idea why Mr. Ormsby brought the jewelry box into the kitchen after you left?"

"Yes," Judson said, with an emphatic nod. "Mr. Ted always gave presents to ladies he no longer wished to see. I'm certain this was a parting gift for Miss Prentiss."

Liz's imagination went into action. She pictured Heather and Ormsby at the kitchen table and Ormsby telling her she'd misunderstood his intentions. Then he took the jewelry box out of his pocket and set it on the table, probably saying he'd enjoyed their Florida fling and wanted her to have a token of his esteem. But Heather refused to accept the gift. While he tried to persuade her to open the box, he drank his coffee. Then suddenly she jumped up and left without even touching the box. That's why her fingerprints weren't on it.

She was pleased with this deduction except for one thing. *How had she managed to pour the medicine into his coffee without him noticing?* Maybe he got up to get sugar, or something, and she seized the chance.

But Eichle had his own spin on it. "The way I see it, Ormsby told her the bad news and then said he had a gift for her," he said. "The jewelry box was in his bedroom. When he went to get it she dumped the medicine into his cup and split."

Liz had to admit this made more sense than Ormsby leaving the table to get sugar. "But isn't it strange that Heather left before Ormsby came back with her gift?" she asked Eichle.

"I agree it's unusual behavior," he replied. "I can't imagine any woman being told she was going to get a gift from a billionaire and not waiting around to see what it was."

"Heather is not your average woman," Liz said. "I think her pride made her leave without waiting to see what Ormsby had for her."

"You're right, she's above average in many ways, but it wasn't her pride that made her leave instead of accepting the gift. The jewelry would have been proof of a relationship between her and Ormsby. She'd just poisoned his coffee. She didn't want to risk creating a tangible link. The D.A. will be glad to get this evidence."

It was great, comparing deductions, Liz thought. But how was Judson reacting to this talk? Just as she glanced at him, he spoke. "Do you believe Miss Prentiss knew she'd put enough medicine in his cup to kill him?"

"Yes, I think she did," Eichle replied.

That would make it premeditated murder, Liz thought. If Heather went on trial she could be sentenced to life in prison, unless her attorney convinced the jury she was insane, in which case she'd end up in a facility for the criminally insane. But she had to agree with Eichle. Heather wasn't out of it all the time. What was her state of mind when she poisoned the coffee?

"Judson, do you recall how much medicine was in the bottle when you went on your day off that morning?" Eichle asked.

"I remember distinctly," Judson replied. "I had the prescription refilled the day before. The bottle was almost full when I took my regular dose that morning."

"When did you take your next dose?"

"When I returned the next day—just before I made Mr. Ted his first coffee."

He'd smudged any fingerprints Heather might have left on the bottle, Liz thought. That's why the bottle wasn't taken as evidence.

"Do you recall how much medicine was in the bottle at the time?" Eichle asked.

"Yes, the level was down considerably. The bottle was only about a quarter full."

"Didn't you think that was strange?"

"Indeed I did. I puzzled over it while I made the coffee, but then…" His voice trembled slightly. "When I found Mr. Ted soon after, I was so distraught I completely forgot about it. If I had remembered I would have mentioned it to the officer who collected the sample of my medicine."

"You would have remembered if I'd asked you about it that morning," Eichle said. "At the time I didn't think the level in the bottle was relevant. When the officer collected the sample he reported seeing the bottle a quarter full. Now you've told me it was almost full when you left the previous morning. Miss Prentiss poured enough into Mr. Ormsby's cup to kill him."

Eichle believed Heather knew exactly what she was doing, Liz decided. "That's a lot of medicine," she said. "Wouldn't he have noticed his coffee tasted strange?"

"I've been wondering about that, myself," Eichle replied. He turned to Judson. "You told me Mr. Ormsby enjoyed experimenting with different kinds of coffee beans and he was accustomed to exotic blends, but I should think that much medicine in a cupful would give it a terrible taste. I'm surprised he didn't put his cup down after the first sip."

"Mr. Ted didn't sip," Judson said. "He always took his coffee in large draughts." His brow knitted for a moment. "I recall now, when I returned that morning the cups were still on the kitchen table. I remember I was surprised to see two, but then I thought perhaps Dr. Hammond had dropped in to see Mr. Ted. He sometimes did that. When I went to wash the cups I noticed one was empty but the other still had some coffee left in it." He gave a deep sigh. "I've done a lot of thinking since Mr. Ted's death. I have no ill feelings towards Miss Prentiss."

Startled, Liz glanced at Eichle. His face, usually devoid of reaction, showed his surprise at Judson's statement. "I was very fond of Mr. Ted," Judson said. "But I've always known he was no saint. He treated women badly. Oh, not that he abused them—he was too much of a gentleman, but I knew he led them to believe he wanted to marry them, then soon tired of them and gave them their walking papers."

"Along with a piece of jewelry as a pacifier," Liz said.

Judson nodded. "But I knew sooner or later there'd be a woman who was different. I knew he'd get his comeuppance one day."

He couldn't have imagined a woman like Heather, Liz thought. Nobody could, least of all Ormsby.

"What's going to happen to Miss Prentiss if she's indicted?" Judson asked.

"There's no predicting the outcome," Eichle replied. "She has a very clever attorney."

Judson shook his head. "As I said before, I bear her no ill will. I've seen Mr. Ted through his love affairs, if you can call them that, since his prep-school years. They always ended with him tiring of the young lady and dropping her like a hotcake. Then when he was in college, that's when he started with the parting gifts. I knew he couldn't go on like that. Something was bound to happen." A sad look came into his eyes.

Liz decided it was time they changed the subject. Even with Judson's lack of rancor towards Heather, this talk must be hard on him. "Do you plan to stay with your sister permanently, Judson?" she asked.

"Yes, but not in her Brooklyn flat. I plan to get a nice large place for us. My sister is a widow and not well-off financially. I intend to go to England to visit relatives and I'll take her with me. She hasn't been back there for many years."

For the remainder of the meal, the talk centered on topics other than the poisoning of Theodore Van Brunt Ormsby. It wasn't till they'd finished dessert that Judson returned to the subject. "Will I be called to testify at Miss Prentiss's hearing?" he asked.

"Yes, but don't let that hold up making your plans to go to England," Eichle replied. "Most likely the hearing will take place very soon."

Eichle seemed pleased, Liz thought. After talking with Judson, he believed he had evidence that Heather was in her right mind when she poisoned the coffee. But she realized all this was speculation. No one except Heather and Ormsby knew what had happened that morning in the penthouse kitchen. The truth was buried with Ormsby and lay deep in Heather's confused mind.

After they'd said goodnight to Judson and seen him off in a cab, Eichle said, "I didn't drive my car tonight. I'll get a taxi and drop you off on my way home."

"Thanks, but I don't want you to go out of your way," Liz replied. She had no idea where Eichle lived. She realized she didn't know much about him except that he lived alone somewhere in Manhattan. Sophie had told her that.

"I'll have to pass your area anyway," he said. "I live as far downtown as you can get."

"Do you live in one of those apartments near the Battery?"

"Yes, so you see dropping you off won't be out of my way at all."

In the cab, she said, "It was a nice evening. But I thought Judson looked frail, didn't you?"

"Yes, I noticed," Eichle replied. "The poor old guy has his health problems, and being arrested didn't do him any good."

Liz knew it wouldn't take long to get from the Plaza to her apartment. She didn't want to spend the entire time talking about Judson. She wanted to know why Eichle hadn't made trouble for her after he found out she'd been getting Homicide information from Sophie. "You bolted out of my place the other night without answering something I asked you," she said.

He seemed unprepared for the sudden change of subject. "What?" he asked. A moment later he said, "Oh, I remember." Though it was too dark in the cab to see his face clearly, she sensed he was frowning. "You must think I'm a vindictive old grouch," he said.

"You sure acted like one for a while," she replied. "But lately I've noticed some improvement."

He laughed. "I was never enough of a grouch to make trouble for you, Rooney, not that I didn't want to. It really bugged me, running into you everywhere I went."

"How do you feel about it now?"

"You showing up at murder scenes with Dan? I still don't like it."

"Well, you don't have to put up with that for a couple of weeks. Dan's on vacation."

"Yeah?" He sounded pleased. "What are you going to do for kicks if there's a major homicide while he's gone?"

"Following homicide cases isn't my only source of entertainment," she retorted. "Besides, going to the murder scene is only part of it." But it ranked high, she thought. However, she wasn't going to let him know that. If an interesting case came up while Dan was away, she didn't want Eichle smugly picturing her frustration.

The taxi stopped in front of her building. She thanked him for the ride.

"I'll see you at Heather's hearing," he said.

His words lingered in her mind as she let herself into her apartment. She'd enjoyed their exchange of ideas on the case tonight, but apparently he was in no hurry for another such talk. It was too early for bed. She picked up the novel she'd almost finished and tried to concentrate on it. She couldn't. She kept recalling tonight's talk. It had been almost as stimulating as the discussion they'd had the night of the shrimp-creole dinner. There'd been a softening of

Eichle's attitude that night. For a while, she'd felt as if they were working together on the case.

With a sharp sense of regret, she realized the chances were slim of this happening again.

TWENTY-ONE

HER PHONE RANG a few minutes after she got to her desk the next morning. It was the D.A.'s office. Heather's hearing was scheduled for tomorrow at nine a.m.

She'd have to tell Dr. Tyrone Jackson that she'd be out of the office for a couple of hours tomorrow morning and she'd have to explain why. Of course he'd be curious. If she wasn't careful she might let it slip that she got into this because of her interest in homicides. She mustn't let him know about that. He'd react the same way as Wade. And if he found out she'd been going to murder scenes with Dan, he'd react the same way as Eichle.

Sophie phoned after lunch. "I guess you've been notified about Heather's hearing," she said. "Have you told Dan's stand-in you're testifying?"

"Not yet. I've been putting it off because I know he'll be curious."

"I'd better hang up and let you get to that, but before I go I have something exciting to tell you. I'm being assigned to Patrol, starting next week. No more filing reports and digging for records. I'll be out there where the action is."

"Great! I know you've been hoping for this," Liz said. Pleased as she was for Sophie, she knew there'd be no more information coming from Homicide about future cases. With Sophie gone, she'd have to muddle along with what she heard on TV or read in the newspapers. Well, at least she could still go to homicide scenes with Dan, she thought. An instant later another thought struck her. Dan was getting close to retirement.

"This takes me one step closer to applying for detective training," Sophie said. "Imagine what I'll be able to tell you when I'm a homicide detective!"

"That will be worth waiting for," Liz replied. It was a bright spot on a far-off horizon, she thought.

"I'm going straight home after work," Sophie said, "but let's meet for coffee tomorrow. You can tell me all about the hearing."

When Liz went to tell Dr. Jackson about her mandatory presence at Heather's hearing, he wasn't in his office. Quitting time came and he still wasn't back. She left him a memo. She had to admit to a feeling of relief. Now she didn't have to explain and run the risk of him knowing she liked to follow murder cases. She'd had enough male disapproval without adding his.

THE NEXT MORNING she took a taxi to the hearing. She wasn't looking forward to it. The prospect of seeing Heather as a prisoner stirred up mixed feelings of compassion and apprehension about the damaging testimony. How would Heather react?

Outside the courtroom she ran into Eichle. "Are you nervous?" he asked.

"A little," she admitted.

"Heather's attorney will try and rattle you," he said. "Don't let him."

She knew the D.A. was counting on her to help nail down Heather's ability to stand trial. She knew she had to tell it like it was, but she didn't want Heather tried like a criminal and sentenced to life in prison or a hospital for the criminally insane. The deaths of her parents and her beloved twin sister had traumatized her and made her the way she was. Her gravely disturbed mind needed intensive therapy if it were ever to heal. She should be given the chance to recover.

Eichle guessed what she was thinking. "I've seen too many killers get off with a slap on the wrist because of alleged insanity," he said. She shook her head. His years of dealing with real criminals had made him cynical. His cynicism had blinded him to Heather's plight.

When they entered the courtroom her first thought was to sit where Heather could see her when she was brought in. A moment later she changed her mind. If Heather smiled at her or waved or gave any sign of recognition, the judge might take this as a normal reaction. He might decide this was something a mentally disturbed person would not do under the circumstances. She sat in the rear of the room where Heather would not immediately see her.

As the proceedings progressed, she knew she needn't have worried. Heather's attorney was extremely clever. His interrogation of the three psychiatrists who'd examined her resulted in statements the D.A. had a hard time trying to dispute. They told the court that Heather was suffering from severe mental trauma brought on by the sudden deaths of her entire family, including the twin sister she adored. Her condition involved disruption of identity, delusion, and depression, they said. They sounded just like that psychiatrist on TV, Liz thought. Then all three stated that since this condition had been brought on by severe shock, her mind could be restored by prolonged psychotherapy and kept stabilized by medication. The opposing testimony of a psychiatrist called by the D.A. was weak.

When the D.A. called Liz to the stand, she glanced at Heather. Would Heather consider her testimony a betrayal? Their eyes met, but Heather didn't seem to recognize her. Liz decided she must be heavily medicated.

The D.A. finished his interrogation. Heather's attorney took over. Though Liz thought the D.A. had done a good job of establishing the fact that Heather knew exactly what she was doing when she locked her in and also had the photo spliced, the attorney made it appear as if these actions were due to identity disruption and delusion. He also said that Heather leaving before Ormsby returned to the kitchen with her gift was further proof of her mental incapacity. Any woman in her right mind would be curious to see what kind of gift she was going to get from a billionaire.

The judge ruled Heather unfit to stand trial and ordered her returned to the hospital for intensive psychotherapy. Her case would be reviewed at a future date.

Liz waited for Eichle in the corridor outside the courtroom. "I'm sorry," she told him. She was, but not because of the outcome of the hearing. She was pleased that Heather had been given a chance to recover, but she knew things hadn't turned out the way he hoped.

"Maybe it's for the best," he said, with a shrug of his shoulders. "Maybe those shrinks can straighten her out. Anyway, it's over for now."

"See you around, Eichle," she said, as they left the courthouse.

"When Dan gets back, maybe," he replied. He had to say that, she thought as she hailed a cab. He had to get in that dig.

To make up for time lost attending the hearing, she didn't go out for lunch. Instead, she sent out for a sandwich and a soda. While eating at her desk, she turned on the TV news channel just in time to catch a bulletin concerning a double murder at the Waldorf Hotel.

Police had been called to the hotel, where a member of the housekeeping staff had discovered the bodies of a man and a woman in a room. Both had been shot. A few minutes later, Sophie phoned. "I didn't get a chance to call you before. Two people were shot and killed at the Waldorf a little while ago."

"I just caught it on TV. Do you know any more details?"

"No. Eichle's gone over there with Lou Sanchez. I won't know anything else till they get back. I'll call you later."

Murder at the Waldorf, she thought, as she hung up the phone. It sounded as intriguing as *The Case of the Poisoned Playboy.* She looked across the hall into Dan's office and saw Dr. Jackson putting on his coat. She knew he was getting ready to go to the murder scene. She felt a pang of frustration.

She kept the TV on for the rest of the afternoon for further details, but nothing new was reported. Sophie phoned shortly before quitting time to say Eichle and Sanchez hadn't returned yet. "Sorry I have nothing to tell you," she said. She added that Ralph's mother was in town and they were taking her out to Staten Island for dinner with the family. "I'll call you tomorrow," she said.

Liz was about to turn off the TV and go home

when a news bulletin came on. The murder victims had been identified, but names were being withheld pending notification of their families. However, the maid who'd come upon the gruesome scene had talked to a news reporter. She didn't recall much because she was very shocked, she said, but she remembered the man's face and he looked familiar. She'd seen him on TV, she said. He was some Washington big shot, she thought. She added that the woman's face wasn't familiar but she looked young enough to be the man's daughter.

Liz gave a deep sigh. What a time for Dan to be on vacation!

As soon as she got home, she turned the TV on to the news channel. She might as well get used to doing this, she thought. In another week Sophie would be riding in a patrol car and soon Dan might decide to retire. With these changes, television and tabloids would become her only resource for following homicide cases.

In the middle of this disheartening thought, the phone rang. She was startled to hear Eichle's voice. "Rooney, I guess you heard about the Waldorf murders."

He'd called to needle her, she thought. "Yes, I heard," she replied.

"I was at the scene all afternoon," he said. "This

one's right up your alley, Rooney. When the names are released, you'll know what I mean."

She already knew what he meant. He was rubbing it in. "Why did you call me, Eichle?" she asked.

"Well, while I was at the scene I got to thinking how interested you'd be in this case, and…"

"And you thought you'd do a little gloating?"

"Let me finish. I'm not gloating."

"Then what *are* you doing?"

"I'm trying to tell you I've been thinking things over," he said. "I have a different slant, now, on your interest in homicides. I'd like to get together with you and discuss this Waldorf case as it goes along."

She was speechless. His voice came into the silence. "Rooney—are you still there?"

"Yes…yes, I'm here."

"Did you hear what I said?"

"Yes. I'm…well, 'surprised' is too mild a word. Whatever happened to 'meddling in police business'?"

"I told you, I've been thinking things over. I liked talking with you about the Ormsby case the night you fed me that great shrimp dinner. I want to discuss this case with you as it develops—and future cases too. So what do you say? Shall we get together soon?"

A few minutes ago she'd been feeling sorry for herself, wishing things didn't have to change. Now she knew change could be positive, especially when it took place in the mind of a man like George Eichle.

"Sure," she replied. "For starters, how about dropping in at my place tomorrow night?"

"I was hoping you'd suggest getting started *tonight*," he said.

* * * * *

REQUEST YOUR FREE BOOKS!

2 FREE NOVELS
PLUS 2 FREE GIFTS!

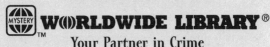

Your Partner in Crime